12

CURL UP AND DYE (BOOK 12)

A HARLEY AND DAVIDSON MYSTERY

LILIANA HART
LOUIS SCOTT

DEDICATION

To our readers—Thank you for loving Hank and Agatha as much as we do.

The Harley and Davidson Mystery Series
The Farmer's Slaughter
A Tisket a Casket
I Saw Mommy Killing Santa Claus
Get Your Murder Running
Deceased and Desist
Malice in Wonderland
Tequila Mockingbird
Gone With the Sin
Grime and Punishment
Blazing Rattles
A Salt and Battery
Curl Up and Dye
First Comes Death Then Comes Marriage
Box Set 1 (Books 1 - 4)
Box Set 2 (Books 5 - 8)

CHAPTER ONE

Wednesday

It was a real scorcher, and the heat was so thick you could chew it while it cooked you from the inside out.

Hank paced back and forth across his lawn, walking a rut into his carefully manicured grass, while sweat trickled down his spine and into his cargo shorts. Good Lord, he'd never get used to the Texas heat, and summer hadn't even started yet.

He looked over at Agatha with a scowl. She sat in the shade of a big elm tree sipping her lemonade without a care in the world. He *hmmph*ed and kept pacing. Little did she know her world was about to be turned upside down. He'd tried to warn her, but she was stubborn as a mule. It served her right, in his opinion.

He rubbed at his stomach, his nerves and the heat making him feel slightly ill.

"Hank," Agatha called out. "Why can't we just wait inside? We might be out here for hours. They didn't even tell us what time they were coming."

"Oh, they're coming," Hank said, almost to himself.

He'd felt the disturbance in the atmosphere. Either aliens had come to invade the planet or his sisters had crossed into Bell County.

On second thought, maybe waiting outside was a bad decision. That made Agatha a sitting duck. She'd never stand a chance.

"Why don't you go back inside where it's cool," he said. "I'll keep watch out here."

"It's not the National Guard," Agatha said, laughing.

"That's what you think." Hank kicked at the ground and then immediately regretted it when a clump of grass shot across the yard. The muscles in his chest began to tighten. Maybe he was having a heart attack. Maybe he was dying. That wouldn't be so bad. He swiped at the sweat dripping from his forehead.

"Why don't you come sit by me," she said. "I've got extra lemonade, and maybe you can explain to me why you're terrified of your sisters."

"I'm not terrified," he said, snapping back. And then he closed his eyes and blew out a breath. "Sorry. I don't mean to take it out on you. But this is a bad idea."

"Come sit and cool off," she said again. "You'll be no good to anyone if you keep standing there worrying to death. And you don't want to be sunburned for the wedding."

"All right, all right," he said, heading toward the elm. He let the tension release from his shoulders and exhaled, long and slow.

"What in the world?" Agatha asked, coming to her feet. "What is that horrible sound?"

"Huh?" Hank asked.

"That noise," she said. "It sounds like a cross between

fingernails down a chalkboard and putting a car in a wood chipper."

Hank stopped to listen, crossing his fingers he heard what Agatha was hearing. Too many years of gunfire and flashbangs had left him with permanent damage, and Agatha had not-so-subtly hinted more than once that he should get hearing aids. But he wasn't old, so he sure as heck wasn't going to get hearing aids.

Then he heard it. And it sounded exactly as Agatha had described. Neighbors were coming out of their houses and standing on the fort porches, looking for the source. The sound grew closer and more offensive, and Hank pulled the Colt .45 from its holster and held it down at his side so as not to alarm the neighbors.

A silver minivan ran a stop sign and squealed around the corner on two wheels, knocking over a trash can and a decorative lion someone had put at the end of their sidewalk.

"Holy smokes," Agatha said. "They must be drunk. I'll call it in. Make sure you get the license plate number."

The van bore down on them, gaining speed, and Hank pushed Agatha toward the front porch so they weren't so close to the street. Smoke blew from the engine of the van, and the windows were tinted almost black. Maybe it was a hit job. Or a bomb. It wasn't impossible that his past had followed him to Texas.

The van swerved as it passed by them and did a U-turn in the middle of the street, leaving black tire marks and a trail of black exhaust. Hank pushed Agatha behind him and aimed his weapon, and then the van drove onto his lawn and came to a sudden stop.

The license plate was hanging off the front by a single

screw, and Hank closed his eyes and said a quick prayer. Pennsylvania plates.

"Please, God, no," he said.

The driver's side door opened and a short, round woman dismounted unceremoniously, waving away the black smoke and coughing. Her hair was steel gray and looked like she'd brushed it with a Brillo pad, and she wore army-green BDUs and a gray T-shirt that said *Armed and dangerous* on the front. Hazel was a good fifteen years older than he was, and she'd never had a problem letting everyone know she was in charge.

"Umm," Agatha said, gripping his arm so tight he thought it might leave bruises. "Is that?"

"Yep," he said.

And then he watched as the passenger door opened. Two bare feet stuck out at him and then his sister Betty hopped out of the van in a swirl of color. The caftan she wore was shades of blue and green, and there were tiny bells sewn in the hem so she tinkled when she moved. Her white-blond hair flowed down her back, and there was a slightly vacant expression on her face.

"Let us out of here," someone said from the back of the van as they pounded on the window.

Betty smiled serenely and pulled open the sliding door. Soda cans tumbled out onto the lawn, and then a bunch of arms and legs fought their way to freedom and Brenda, Patsy, and Gayle stood before him, looking a little the worse for wear and not at all happy about it.

"Good Lord," Patsy said, fanning her shirt. "Would it kill you to get air-conditioning in that thing? I thought I was going to have a stroke."

"Oh, hush up," Brenda said. "At least you didn't have to sit by it. Last time I was next to anything that dead was

Arthur's funeral. Dead as a doornail. But didn't look that much different when he was living."

"That's true," Gayle said. "I could never tell if Arthur was dead or alive half the time." She patted her freshly permed locks and stretched her arms high above her head, and then she bent at the waist and touched her toes. "I stuck a fork in his hand during the Thanksgiving of '95 just to make sure."

"I remember that," Brenda said, nodding her head. "He was in one of those turkey comas so it was kind of hard to tell. I do miss that man. We had some good times."

Hank let the conversation rush over him. There was no stopping it, and he'd learned the best way to deal with them was let them run out of steam.

"Hank Davidson," Hazel barked. "Where are your manners? Aren't you even going to tell us hello?"

Hank took a deep breath and squeezed Agatha's hand. "Hello, Hazel. How was your drive?"

She harrumphed and they all started talking again. He had no idea what had happened, but he heard *flat tire* and *Cracker Barrel*, and something about gunshots that made him terrified for whoever had the misfortune of running into his sisters. And then they all rushed him and threw their arms around him.

"Sweet little Hank," Betty said, stroking his cheek like he was a baby. Of all his sisters, Betty had been the one to give him the least amount of grief over the choices he'd made in life. But as their chatter rolled over him all the old resentments came rising to the surface. They'd never forgiven him for marrying Tammy. They'd never considered her good enough, and had told him at the time he was making the biggest mistake of his life. They hadn't been nice, to him or to Tammy, and none of them had even bothered to show up to her funeral. Betty had sent flowers.

That was a hard thing to forgive, and he guessed he still had some forgiving to do because the anger hadn't passed with the time. And he fully expected them to treat Agatha the same way they'd treated Tammy.

"Oh, you're too thin," Brenda said, checking him over like he was a turkey at Thanksgiving. "Is nobody feeding you?" She scowled at Agatha.

"Poor thing," Gayle said. "Who let you leave the house like this? You're all wrinkled. I'll press all your shirts while I'm here since no one is doing it for you. And honeybear, stop wearing socks with your sandals."

Hank felt his blood pressure spike, and he saw all the neighbors were still standing on their porches watching the show. His lips thinned and his eyes scanned his sisters, lingering over each of them as they clucked over him and shot poisonous verbal darts at Agatha. And then his eyes rested on Hazel. She'd been quiet, standing back from the others and watching him closely. But it wasn't the scowl on her face that drew his attention. It was the blooming shiner on her eye.

"What happened to your eye?" he asked, appalled at the sight.

"Long story," she said. "Why don't you introduce us to your friend?"

"This is my fiancée," Hank said, emphasizing the word. "Agatha Harley. Agatha, these are my sisters. Hazel is the oldest. And then there's Betty, Brenda, Patsy, and Gayle."

"Nice to meet you all," Agatha said. He could feel the nervous energy coming off her in waves, and his sisters didn't help the tension any. They just stared at her."

6

"So you think you're going to marry our baby brother, huh?" Gayle asked.

"I am going to marry him," Agatha said, straightening her shoulders. "In two weeks. We're glad you've decided to come celebrate with us."

Hazel snorted. "We'll see about that. Two weeks is a long time. People change their minds all the time."

"I won't change my mind," Agatha said.

"I wasn't talking about you," Hazel said.

"Hazel," Hank said. "This is our home, and you're welcome here as long as you treat both of us with respect."

"Well," Patsy huffed. "I never heard such a thing. I thought Southerners were supposed to be polite. Blood runs thicker than water. Don't you forget that."

"Blood doesn't mean anything to me," Hank said. "I've learned over the years that family is what you make it. And I've made my family here."

"If you don't want us here then we'll turn right around and head back home," Hazel said.

"Not likely," Betty said with a good-natured smile. "I'm not getting back in that van until it's fumigated and I get a good night's sleep. I'm too old for road trips. Stop being an instigator, Hazel. We voted and we're all sick of your attitude. You didn't want to come to begin with."

"You voted?" Hazel asked, narrowing her eyes at her sisters. "Why would I want to come watch Hank make another mistake?"

"Because we voted on that too," Gayle said. "Majority rules."

Hank growled low in his throat and was about to lose his temper, but Agatha squeezed his arm.

"I don't mean to interrupt this touching family reunion," Brenda said. "But don't you think we have more important things to talk about than Hank's next marriage? We've got a bit of a crisis on our hands, and Hank is the law. He'd probably know what to do about this mess."

"What mess?" Hank asked, sharper than he'd intended.

He heard another squeal of tires, and a bright red convertible sped down the street and came to a stop in front of their house. He closed his eyes and decided to accept that the universe was against him today. He might as well go back to bed and wake up with a fresh start tomorrow. That was the only way he'd make it through.

Heather Cartwright's bleached blond hair shone like a beacon and rock and roll blasted from the speakers.

Hazel snorted. "Figures she'd be consorting with women like that. Now we know how she got her hooks into Hank."

The others nodded in agreement and watched Heather get out of the car like she was a car wreck. Though to be fair, Heather was a bit of a car wreck. But she'd never much cared what people thought about her.

"Agatha!" Heather squealed. "I found the cutest little boutique in Austin for your trousseau. Lots of lingerie. I promise you'll thank me, Hank. Let's go shopping."

"I can't right now," Agatha said. "We've got company."

"But the wedding is only two weeks away," Heather said, pouting. "It's the little things that will add up in the end. Believe me. I'm an expert."

"Yeah, go along and go shopping," Gayle said. "It's not like his family traveled all this way to get a look at you."

Heather arched a brow at the tone and put her hands on her hips. "If you only came to get a look at her then you can do it at the wedding. Good grief, Hank. This is your family? Is your last name Manson?"

"Heather," Hank said, a warning note in his voice. "You're not helping."

"Maybe it's time for us to go, girls," Brenda said. "I want to check into the hotel and soak in the hot tub. I've got to get the death cooties off me."

Hank regretted even asking the question. "What death cooties?"

"Tell him," Betty said to Hazel. "He can help."

"Help with what?" Hank asked.

"Him," Hazel said, pointing to the third-row seat.

They all moved in a huddle until they could see into the van and the third row. There was a man sitting in the back seat, his head lolled to one side and his face waxy and pale with death. He also appeared to be naked. Hank felt the blood drain out of his face and he looked between his sisters and the body they'd been transporting.

"Somebody had better start explaining right now," he said.

"Hey, you're the big-shot detective," Hazel said. "Doesn't seem so hard to figure out to me. I'm more concerned about the fella I shot. That seems like something that would come with a lot of paperwork."

"You were in a shoot-out?" Agatha asked, pulling out her phone.

Hank examined the big swollen purple patch of traumatized skin around Hazel's right eye. It had blistered into hues of blue and green over the course of their conversation.

"Enough of this," Hank demanded. "Start talking or I'm hauling you all down to the sheriff's office. How'd you get that black eye?"

"It's his fault," Hazel said, pointing to the dead guy.

"Are you telling me that's a real person in your van? An actual dead man?"

They looked at him like he was the one who'd lost his mind. "Of course it's a real dead person," Patsy said. "He fell right out of the hearse."

"Oh God," he heard Agatha say.

Brenda and Gayle had gotten back in the van and pulled the dead man out onto the lawn. "I'm not riding with him over to the hotel," Brenda said.

"Are you telling me this man fell out of a hearse, and instead of stopping and calling the police, you picked him up and put him in your van?"

"We had to," Betty said defensively. "Those men were shooting at us. If Hazel hadn't shot back we'd probably all be dead."

The others were nodding in agreement.

"It all happened very fast," Brenda said.

"Wow," Heather said. "Some family, Hank."

"Heather," Agatha said. "Not now."

"Heather," Hank said. "You leave now unless you want to become part of another murder investigation. Agatha, call 911 and get Coil here ASAP. And you five start talking, and you'd better be telling the truth or I'm going to arrest you all."

"We did not raise you to behave this way, Hank Davidson," Gayle said. "It is clear to me this woman has been a bad influence on you."

"That's my cue to go," Heather said, and trotted back to her car as fast as her spiked heels would carry her.

Hank was glad Agatha had moved away from the group so she could make phone calls. His head pounded, from the heat and the chaos, and he walked away from the circle of women and went to stand over the body. He could deal with the dead. It was the living who were the problem.

"Umm...Hank," his neighbor from across the street said.

"Maybe you could drape this over the...umm...you know." She swallowed and tried not to look at the corpse in his yard. "There's kids on this street."

"I'm sorry about this," he said, taking the sheet from her.

"You definitely made the neighborhood more interesting since you moved here," she said. Hank didn't even know what her name was, but clearly she knew him. "Most exciting thing that ever happened before you was forty years ago when Wally Tabor fell off his roof and broke his neck dressed like Santa. Congratulations on the wedding, by the way. We're real excited about it."

Hank wondered who else was coming to their wedding. Probably the whole town. "Thanks," he said. "And thanks for the sheet. I'll get it back to you."

Her eyes got big and she pursed her lips. "You can keep it, honey."

"Right," Hank said, and went to cover the body.

Spots danced in front of his eyes and the heat from the sun was oppressive. It rose from the ground in waves and pressed from above like a laser. He'd lived in Texas two years, and he still wasn't used to the heat. They were still having snow in Philadelphia.

"You don't look so good," Agatha said, coming up next to him. "Why don't you go inside with your sisters and I'll wait out here for Coil to arrive. He's on the way now."

"Thanks," he said.

"I'm sorry I pressed about having your family here," she said. "I never want to hurt you or put more stress on you than you already carry. I didn't realize."

"I should have told you why things were so bad in the first place," he said. "You only knew what I told you. And maybe it's not such a bad thing. One way or another, maybe I can put hard feelings aside. How they choose to behave is up to them. But I want to go into our future together with as little baggage as possible."

She nodded and leaned up to kiss him. "Go on inside before they get too impatient. I can't decide if they want to kidnap you or kill you."

Hank laughed. "Probably a little of both. Let me know when Coil gets here."

He walked back to his sisters and herded them toward the front door. "Come on," he said. "You'll be more comfortable in the house with the air conditioner while we wait for Coil to get here. Anyone want a drink?"

"I'll take a vodka tonic," Gayle said, taking a seat on the couch. "I need to cool down."

"Oh, that sounds good. Be a dear and get me one too," Patsy said.

"I've got water and iced tea," he said patiently. "No vodka."

"You always were a strange one," Betty said, clucking her tongue.

"You want me to hang outside with skinny?" Patsy asked. "I've already got lots of theories, and I'd like to see this investigation through." She was a true-crime fanatic, and Hank only hoped she didn't disturb any evidence.

"Agatha can handle it until Coil gets here," he said.

"You keep talking about Coil," Brenda said. "Who's Coil?"

"Reggie Coil," Hank said. "He's the sheriff in Bell County."

Gayle gasped and put her hand on her chest. "I saw his picture in the paper a couple of months ago. He looks just like Brad Pitt. Oh, I can't wait to meet him. He's a hottie."

"Is he married?" Brenda asked.

"Yes," Hank said. "He's very married."

"That never mattered much to you before," Hazel said, elbowing her sister.

"Hush, Hazel," Brenda said. "That was a low time for me. It was right after Arthur died, and a woman has needs."

"Oh, for the love of..." Hank said, but his sisters started talking all at once again. He let out a loud whistle and everyone went silent.

"Everyone sit down and be quiet," he said. "No one is leaving this room until I find out exactly what happened, who the dead guy is, and who was shooting what. Where's Patsy?"

"She slipped out the back while you were distracted," Betty said. "She's in the front yard with that woman you're marrying. You know she's not going to miss a chance to work this case from start to finish. You really should have more pride in your appearance, Hank. No one wears Hawaiian shirts. It's not the eighties."

"I do," he said. "And I'm retired. Kind of. So I can wear what I want. We've got more important things to worry about than what I'm wearing."

"Good point," Hazel said, looking out the window at Patsy and Agatha. "You think Agatha is going to punch her?"

"I've got ten dollars on Patsy," Brenda said. "She's scrappy."

"Deal," Hazel said.

CHAPTER TWO

Patience wasn't Agatha's strong suit, and the temptation to lift the sheet and get a good look at the body was getting stronger the longer she waited for Coil to arrive.

She'd waved the neighbors all back inside, but she could feel their eyes on her as she shuffled closer to the bed-sheeted corpse. She checked her watch again and blew out a breath. The scene was already ruined to heck and back, so it's not like she could do much more damage. Especially if she was only looking.

Agatha crept up to the body, looked both ways down the street, and then squatted down next to the body and started to lift the sheet.

"Are you allowed to do that?" a voice said behind her.

Agatha dropped the sheet and looked over her shoulder guiltily.

"I'm Patsy," the woman said. "Hank's sister."

"Yes, I remember," Agatha said.

"Did you secure the scene?" Patsy looked up and down the street like Agatha had and then squatted down next to her. "Go on then, let's take a look. I've been dying to check him out ever since we got him loaded in the van. But they didn't let me sit next to him. Hurry, girl. They'll be out here any minute. Hank can only keep them preoccupied for so long."

Agatha looked back over her shoulder toward the house and saw several faces in the window.

"They're looking, aren't they?" Patsy asked, clucking her tongue. "Old busybodies."

The sound of sirens was growing louder in the distance and Agatha breathed out a sigh of relief. She looked at Patsy, thinking they'd take a step back and let Coil take control, but clearly Patsy had other ideas. Patsy's elbow shot out and connected with her ribs, and Agatha *oof*ed as she sprawled backward on the ground.

"Hey!" Agatha said.

"Out of the way, skinny," Patsy said. "I've got a crime to solve."

"You've got some reality to check," Agatha said, her brows raised. She slowly got to her feet and tried to take a calming breath.

Patsy blew a raspberry and peeked under the sheet. "I'm an old lady. Whatcha going to do? Fight me?"

"No," Agatha said. "But if you touch that body, you're going to find yourself with a mouth full of dirt and your hands behind your back."

"Been there, done that, sugar. You should've met my husband. He was a real pistol."

Coil chose that opportune moment to pull in front of the house in his truck, and another cruiser and an ambulance were right behind him.

Agatha blew out a breath of relief and grabbed Patsy by the arm, pulling her to her feet unceremoniously.

Coil looked at her like she was half crazy, but she didn't

care. "Good to see you," she called out. She and Coil hadn't always seen eye to eye, but they were friends, and right now, he was the only ally she had. "Patsy here is an amateur detective."

"Ahh," Coil said, nodding his head. "I don't think we've had the pleasure of meeting."

"Patsy Davidson," she said, holding out a hand. "I'm Hank's sister. You single?"

Coil grinned, and Agatha shook his head. Coil was well aware of his looks and knew how to use them to his advantage. "No, ma'am. Happily married for going on eighteen years now."

"Your wife, is she healthy? No sickness? Bad hips or knees?"

"She's perfect," Coil said, but he was clearly taken aback.

"Huh," Patsy said. "I got two new hips last year. Titanium. I can practically swivel a hundred and eighty degrees."

"I'm sure that's very helpful," he said. "Why don't we take a look at this fella in the yard and see what's what?"

Agatha explained how the dead man had come to be in their front yard, and to Coil's credit, he didn't even flinch.

She could practically feel Hank's judgment coming at her in waves from the house. He hadn't wanted to invite his sisters, and she hadn't realized how deep their family feud went. If Hank had only told her what had happened, she wouldn't have insisted on inviting them.

She'd grown up as an only child. Agatha had no family to call her own, and the thought of Hank having five sisters seemed like a good way for her to have an immediate family. But the thought of family had been something that had consumed her whole life. It had only been her and her parents growing up. No big extended family or reunions to look forward to.

And then there was the daughter she'd given up for adoption at birth. It had been a painful time, and it was still a painful memory, and now that her daughter was of adult age, she could request they meet. But she hadn't followed through with the state's office of child welfare about making contact. Sometimes the past was best left in the past. Her daughter had two parents who loved her and raised her. And Agatha was about to start a new life with Hank.

If they managed to make it through the next two weeks. She felt a hand on her shoulder and leaned back into Hank with a sigh. She guessed he hadn't been able to contain his sisters any longer.

"What we need to be talkin' about," Gayle said as she joined the crowd on the lawn, "is a bachelorette party. You don't really get to know someone until you see them at a bachelorette party. Look at that tattoo. That's good artistry right there."

"I was admiring it when we hauled him off the ground and into the van," Betty agreed. "I've been thinking of getting one myself."

"What you want is a tramp stamp," Brenda said. "You don't get too wrinkled back there, so you keep the integrity of the design."

"That's good thinking," Betty said. "We should all get matching tattoos for Agatha's bachelorette party."

"I'm not much on parties," Agatha said, but she didn't think anyone was listening. "And I've already got a tattoo."

"What?" Hank asked, turning her to face him.

"I've already got a tattoo," Agatha said.

"Where? Of what?"

Agatha winked and said, "We've got to save something for our wedding night."

She could tell she'd rendered Hank speechless, and she almost laughed out loud. This whole situation was a comedy of errors.

"We can go without her," Brenda said. "Marriages have a tendency to be less permanent than tattoos."

Hank's sisters cackled with laughter, and Agatha felt her temper go from simmer to full steam.

"It's not worth it," Hank said, putting his hands back on her shoulders to hold her back. Deputies James and Springer had finished up with the body and were helping get him loaded for transport.

"If I could take a moment of your time," Coil said, looking around the circle of women and then to Hank and Agatha. He gave them all a winning smile.

"This is exactly why he's the politician and I'm not," Hank whispered, making her grin.

"Hello ladies," Coil said. "How's it going?"

"Much better now, honey," Gayle said. "You look like the kind of man who could appreciate a little ink. I bet you've got a few."

"Not a one," Coil said.

"Y'all hush up," Patsy said. "The sheriff is trying to get to the bottom of this crime. He's got a job to do, and it's my duty as a citizen to assist in any way. I'd appreciate it if you'd go ahead and deputize me. I already got my gun. Just need a badge."

"I'd be careful of taking a gun over state lines," Coil said, trying to maintain the smile.

"It's all right," she said. "I've got one of those universal passes. I take it everywhere. Don't worry about the badge. The government red tape isn't worth it. I'll just work in an unofficial capacity."

"I need to start taking statements about what happened, and I need one from each of you individually. My deputies are going to help me with that."

"I'm the oldest and I shot that man," Hazel said, "so I think it's only fitting that the sheriff interview me directly instead of pawning me off. You girls can have those other two."

Hank's sisters looked collectively toward Deputies James and Springer, and no one seemed too impressed to have their statements taken by them.

"Let's just get this over with," Brenda said. "I never got my drink, and I'm in desperate need of one." She and Betty went over to the two deputies and started talking, and Springer and James looked like deer caught in the headlights.

Patsy didn't look like she was going anywhere. She pulled a notepad and pen out of her purse and went to stand by Coil.

"I can write in shorthand," she said. "I'll document. You just ask the questions."

Coil pursed his lips, but must've decided it wasn't worth the battle. "Where did you come across the body?

"Not too far," Hazel said. "I guess we've had him in the car a good twenty minutes."

"So you were probably in Bell County," Coil said.

Hazel brightened as Patsy was furiously documenting the conversation word for word.

"Oh, I know we were in Bell County," Hazel said, nodding. "We'd just passed the *Now Entering Bell County*

19

sign, and Brenda commented because it looked like someone had taken a baseball bat to it. It was all crooked and dented up."

"I know the one," Coil said. "Good observation."

Hazel actually looked like she was trying to smile. Agatha hadn't seen anything but a scowl from Hank's oldest sister since she'd arrived.

"That's a good place to start," Coil said. "Why don't you tell me what happened after you came into the county."

"Well," Hazel said, "I was driving because everyone else drives too slow, and it's my van. I passed a cop in the last town, and I think he got me on his radar, so I hurried up so I could get in the next county. In my experience, giving cops a potential of a lot of paperwork keeps them off your back."

"Hmm," Coil said, looking at Hank with a raised brow.

"So I'm going along at a pretty good clip, and I come up on this hearse," Hazel continued. "I was about to pass them when the back door just swung open and a naked man fell out right in the middle of the road. He took a good bounce off the hood while I was slamming on the brakes, and then he kind of shot forward like one of those crash test dummies. And the brakes on Ol' Justine aren't what they used to be, so we rolled right over him, and he kind of got stuck under the wheel."

"Then what happened?" Hank asked.

Agatha wanted to know too. Talk about truth being stranger than fiction.

"There wasn't any traffic and we were parked kind of caddywompas, so Patsy got out to see what was what. She's not squeamish at all. She watches all those serial killer documentaries."

"What did the hearse do?" Coil asked, trying to keep things moving.

"That's what I'm telling ya," Hazel said. "Those fellas sitting in the back of the hearse looked real surprised when the dead guy fell out, and I could see them yelling and waving their arms. The driver slammed on the brakes and the guys in the back went tumbling donkey over elbow out the back. They weren't wearing seat belts." She pinched her lips together disapprovingly.

Coil's lips twitched. "I bet that was real scary for y'all."

"That wasn't the scary part," Hazel said. "I've run over lots of people. The two guys that fell out the back were kind of rattled so they sat there a minute. But the two guys in front got out and looked like they were mad enough to spit nails. They were all dressed like the people in that movie." She snapped her fingers a couple of times. "The one with Will Smith and the aliens."

"*Men in Black*?" Agatha asked.

"Yep, that's the one," Hazel said.

"I love that movie," Patsy said, continuing with her shorthand. "But get to the good part, Hazel. I'm sweatin' like a Baptist in a dance hall."

"Right," Hazel said. "Well, they all started yelling in some funny language, and then the driver pulls out a gun plain as day."

"No way!" Agatha said with a gasp.

"Don't interrupt," Hazel said. "This is the good part. All I can say is it's a good thing I had my handbag." She held the handbag in question up and shook it.

It looked more like a piece of luggage than a handbag to Agatha.

"Why's that?" Coil asked cautiously.

"Because I've got old Jimmy Dickens in here," Hazel said.

"I'm so confused," Hank said softly.

"Jimmy Dickens is my .44 revolver," she said. "I threw open my door and took cover just like they do on the shows. When he raised his gun, I was ready. *Kapow!* He got a shot off, but it pinged off the front of the car. He was a terrible shot. I got him center mass, just like they taught me in my class."

"Oh God," Hank said, rubbing his hand over his face.

"You shot a man center mass with a .44?" Coil asked.

"I've got the proof right here," she said, pointing to her black eye. "Jimmy Dickens always did kick like a mule. It's not my first shiner."

"What happened next?" Coil asked.

"I think it surprised them," Hazel said.

"I imagine so," Agatha said dryly. Most criminals probably didn't expect for seventy-year-old women to fire large handguns in their direction.

"The bullet didn't take him down," Hazel said. "He was pretty tough. The other three helped him get back in the hearse and then they drove away. They were gone, lickety split. I don't know much about gunshot wounds, but if I was them I'd have headed straight to a hospital."

"I'll have my guys check," Coil said. "What direction did they go?"

"They just kept driving straight," she said, shrugging.

"You said they spoke a foreign language?" Coil asked. "Any idea where they were from?"

"Nope," Hazel said. "They looked like bad guys. They all had dark hair, and that swarthy European look."

"Did the men act like the body was important?" Coil asked. "I mean, did it seem like they might have pushed the body out, or did it fall out by accident?"

"It was definitely an accident," she said. "The guys in

the back tried to reach for him, and they sure did look surprised when that door swung open."

"You think you can show us where this happened?" Coil asked.

"Sure, but I'm not riding in the back of a cop car," Hazel said. "Been there, done that."

CHAPTER THREE

"You sure this is the spot?" Hank asked Hazel from the rear seat of Coil's pickup truck. Agatha was next to him, and Hazel sat snug as a bug in the plush leather passenger seat of Coil's truck.

"Do you think I could ever forget where I almost died?" she asked.

"No, I'm sure you wouldn't," Hank said.

Coil grabbed his police radio and called out to Springer and James to position their police vehicles about a half mile on each side of the scene and put out cones. Traffic was light, so things would be kept moving in the far lane. Lieutenant Maria Rodriguez was carrying Hank's other sisters.

Hank wasn't a fan of sitting in the back seat either, and he hopped out of the truck before Coil had stopped all the way. He helped Agatha climb down, and then reached out for Hazel, and they all gathered in front of Coil's truck.

"Listen up," Coil said to everyone. "This is going to be like looking for a needle in a haystack. We had two weapons fired. One of the bullets hit its target, but the other could be anywhere. Look for casings, skid marks, skin, or blood. And anything else that we can take as evidence. We've got a man with a bullet in him running around somewhere. I want updates on hospitals with anyone who was admitted with a GSW. Let's get this done before traffic picks up and people start throwing stuff at us."

While curious motorists crawled by in the opposing lane, Deputy James clicked pics, and the other deputies combed the area. Hank wasn't optimistic, but he took a second look at a set of skid marks.

"There we go," Hank said. "I think I've got something here. Skid marks."

"How can you tell?" Agatha asked.

"See the continuous line of rubber left on the road?" Hank pointed.

"Sure," Agatha said.

"Now see where the line stops for about a foot and then starts up again?"

"Oh," Agatha said, understanding the space was where the body had gotten stuck.

"Good thing he was dead first," Hazel said. "Otherwise that would've hurt real bad."

"Okay," Coil said. "We've got a point of origin. Hazel, can you show us the locations of the men and the hearse from here?"

"I'll try," she said.

On Hazel's instructions, Springer laid down markers so everyone could get a clearer picture.

The heat was brutal, and Hank wished he'd thought to bring a bottle of water with him. The pavement was steaming and the scent of asphalt was nauseating. Little spots were dancing in front of his eyes, and he leaned against the truck when his knees started getting weak.

"You okay?" Agatha asked.

"Yeah," Hank said. "Just hot."

"Summer hasn't even started yet," Agatha said. "That Yankee skin will eventually toughen up."

"Thanks," Hank said. "Very helpful."

"It's been a long morning," she said. "You'll feel better once we get something to eat."

"Got it," Lieutenant Rodriguez said. "Hearse skid marks."

Hank stood upright, and he and Agatha walked to Rodriguez.

"Yikes," Rodriguez said, "You don't look so good. I didn't realize a person could get that pale. Give it another ten years or so, and you'll get used to the heat."

"Everyone's a comedian today," Hank said. He looked down to give his eyes a break from the bouncing glare of the sun, and something glinted in his periphery. He walked over and saw the brass half buried in the roadside dirt. It was a bullet casing. From the size of it, possibly a 9mm semiautomatic.

"Hank?" Coil called out.

"Yeah?" Hank asked.

"You've been staring at the ground a long time. You about to fall over, or did you find buried treasure?"

"Both," Hank said. "Grab an evidence bag."

Coil handed him a bottle of water and bent down to look where Hank was pointing.

"Is that a bullet casing?" Coil asked.

"Dollars to donuts," Hank said. "What are the odds?"

"Maybe our luck is changing," Coil said. He placed his ink pen inside the brass casing so he wouldn't contaminate potential fingerprints before dropping it into an evidence bag.

26

"I got blood, I got blood," Patsy called out, bouncing in her thick-soled shoes.

"You sure, Pats?" Hank asked.

Patsy put her hands on her hips and glared at Hank. "I know blood when I see it. I took an online class."

Hank looked down at the spot on the road where Patsy was pointing, and he was pleasantly surprised to see Patsy's online class had paid off. How it had survived the traffic was a miracle, but so was the fact that his sisters had survived a gunfight with body-snatching outlaws.

"Nice work," Agatha told Patsy, but Patsy ignored her.

Hank saw Agatha deflate, but he couldn't say he was surprised. He'd been through this before, but Agatha was innocent to his sisters' jealousy and pettiness. She didn't deserve to be treated that way, and it made him angry that Agatha was the one getting hurt in all this. Hank had learned a long time ago that his sisters were what they were. They didn't want to change. They didn't want a real family that included all the spouses. They'd even treated their own spouses like outlaws instead of in-laws, and he'd vowed back then not to put up with it.

"Springer," Coil said. "Let's get samples of the blood and get it sent over to the lab. And have this casing tested for prints." He passed over the evidence bag.

"I'm not sure what else we could hope to find," Hank said to Coil. "Maybe we could wrap this up and take it back to the office."

"You're looking pretty piqued," Coil said. "Must be some wedding jitters."

"What?" Agatha asked, looking between Hank and Coil.

"He's kidding," Hank said. "I need food and drink or things are going to get ugly."

"10-4, buddy," Agatha said.

Hazel joined her sisters in Rodriguez's SUV for the ride back to Rusty Gun, and Agatha hopped in the back of Hank's truck and let him take the front seat for the ride back to the sheriff's office.

"So this is a weird case," Agatha said, broaching the topic. "Any ideas what in the world is going on?"

"Definitely weird," Hank said. "Could be former military. Could be mercenaries. I'll have to check the FBI and see if they've got any foreigners they're keeping an eye on."

"I can agree that they were unfamiliar with the area, but how do you get military?" Agatha asked. "They just got schooled by a seventy-year-old woman."

"Their similar dress suggests teamwork and anonymity," Hank explained. "And they all were geared into aggressively approaching the target, or what they perceived as a threat. They probably underestimated Hazel whipping out a cannon, but it doesn't discount the way they responded. I mean the guy got hit with a .44 and it didn't drop him."

"Maybe he was wearing a bulletproof vest," Coil suggested.

"Possibly," Hank said. "Good idea."

"Who could mercenaries be working for in Bell County?" Agatha asked.

"It could be anyone from the government or a drug cartel," Hank said.

"Maybe they were speaking Spanish and Hazel didn't recognize it," Agatha said.

"Possibly," Hank agreed. "They're definitely not locals, whoever they are."

"You're thinking cartels?" Coil asked.

"Not sure. It's going to depend on who the corpse is and what's inside of him."

"Inside?" Agatha asked. "Why in the world would there be anything inside of him?"

"Why else would they steal the body?" Coil asked. "It's not uncommon for the cartels to use bodies to transport drugs or cash. I sent James to the coroner's office so he could observe the autopsy."

"Maybe we should go there too," Hank said. "I've got a feeling."

"I thought you had hunger?" Agatha asked.

"I could eat a taco or two," Hank said. "But the hair is standing up on the back of my neck."

"Never a good sign," Coil said, blowing out a breath. "To the coroner's office we go."

"Wait a sec," Hank said. "Let's think this backward. We've got a hearse and a dead body. Where are our bad guys going to find both of those things?"

"A funeral home," Agatha said.

"Bingo," Hank said.

"Sweet Dreams Funeral Home," he and Coil said together.

"That funeral home has been around forever, and they're the only one for miles," Agatha said. "But there have been lots of rumors over the years of financial problems."

"Funeral homes are good fronts for smuggling," Coil said.

"Let's pay them a visit," Hank said. "See what you can find out about the funeral home from public records."

Agatha was a champion at research, and he knew she'd have the information before he or Coil could even make the attempt.

"It says here that the Sweet Dreams Funeral Home is a hundred-year-old family owned business. Every one of the

Hartley men were certified morticians except the current owner, Brad Hartley."

"Maybe he's squeamish about the dead," Hank said.

"Nope," Coil and Agatha said together.

"Brad's a playboy," Agatha said. "I was surprised as heck that he'd even been left the funeral home when his dad died. Brad's never worked an honest day in his life."

Coil blew out a breath. "I hate to say it, because Brad and I grew up together, but that's pretty much the truth. He likes to party and do drugs and spend his parents' money."

"Which eventually runs out unless you figure out a way to replace it," Hank said.

"I can't see him being involved in smuggling," Coil said. "He's an idiot. No way he's smart enough to pull off something like this."

"People do all kinds of things when they're desperate," Hank said.

CHAPTER FOUR

The Sweet Dreams Funeral Home was an ugly brown brick two-story house on the outskirts of town. Agatha's parents had both been prepared for burial there, and she hadn't driven by the place since then. It hadn't changed much other than the landscaping out front.

The front door was unlocked, and they walked into a plush lobby of dark grained wood panel and maroon carpeting. The air conditioner was on full blast, and it was cold enough to have her teeth chattering. Marble stands held floral arrangements along the walls and painted portraits of the Hartley men hung on the right side of two large white doors leading into the chapel.

"Where is everybody?" Hank asked.

"This place never gets less creepy," Coil said.

"Do you hear that?" Agatha asked. "It sounds like someone is having a disagreement."

The whispers were hushed, but urgent, and it sounded like several people talking at once. When someone yelled out *dead man*, Hank and Coil both drew their weapons and held them at the ready.

31

Agatha stepped behind both of them. There was no need placing herself in danger. She was getting married in two weeks.

The excited chatter grew louder as they approached, and Coil motioned for them to step into a small office while he moved toward the door where the whispers were coming from.

He knocked loudly and said, "Sheriff's office. You in there, Brad? It's Coil. Its business hours, and the door was wide open."

The voices stopped. There was the scrape of what sounded like chairs across the floor and several hissed whispers. She knew Coil had given the reminder of it being business hours so he didn't have to ask for entry.

"Brad, you've got paying customers out here," Coil said. He looked at Hank and shrugged. They'd eventually all be customers one day.

"Coming in," Coil said, out of patience. He opened the door and they came face to face with Hank's sisters.

"Huh," Patsy said. "Some detective you are. We didn't think you were ever going to get here."

"What in the world are you doing here?" Hank bellowed.

Agatha raised her brows. She'd never heard Hank raise his voice. It didn't matter how harrowing the circumstance, Hank always kept his cool. If the look on Coil's face was anything to go by, he was just as surprised as Agatha was.

"It's the next logical place to investigate," Patsy said. "Hearse. Dead guy. Funeral home. Bing, bang, boom. Of course, we weren't expecting to find another body."

"What?" Agatha asked, looking around the room. Sure enough, wedged under a big oak table was a body lying in a pool of blood.

"That's Brad Hartley," Coil said, reaching for his radio. "Did y'all call 911?"

"We were going to," Patsy said. "But then we figured it might be better to call Hank. That's what we were arguing about."

"Please tell me you haven't touched anything," Coil said.

"Of course not," Patsy said, insulted.

"Technically, that's not true," Hazel said. "We touched the door when we came in, and Brenda straightened that picture frame in the hallway. And Gayle looked in the refrigerator before we saw the body on the floor."

"I was thirsty," Gayle said defensively.

Hank closed his eyes and muttered, "For the love of all that's holy. Everyone get out of this room and into the foyer. Don't touch anything else."

Agatha had never seen Hank look so angry, and the vein in his temple bulged. She rubbed her hand across his back and hoped he remembered to breathe at some point before his eyes popped out of their sockets.

"You watch your tone with us, Hank Davidson," Hazel said, placing her hands on her hips. "You can't order us around."

"You see this?" Hank asked, showing her his badge. "When you mess with a crime scene then I can order you wherever I want. And you're this close to being ordered back to Philadelphia."

The sisters all gasped in unison.

"You wouldn't dare," Brenda squeaked.

"Rude," Gayle said.

"We raised you better than that," Betty said.

"Has she changed you so much you don't even have basic manners anymore?" Hazel asked, narrowing her eyes at Agatha. "I guess that's what's to be expected marrying a girl half your age. You should be ashamed of yourself."

"As much as I appreciate the comment," Agatha said, her temper held in check because she knew one of them was going to have to be rational so Coil didn't throw them all in jail, "I'm not half Hank's age. And I've had about enough of the snide comments and rude remarks. We're very well suited, we love each other, and we're getting married in two weeks. Whether you're there or not is up to you. By my definition, family loves each other unconditionally without judgment or reservation. Hank and I have long since passed into adulthood, and you're welcome here as long as you can abide by our wishes and be respectful. If you feel you can't, then we'll understand your absence."

Four of the five sisters stared at her with their mouths hanging open, but Hazel was glaring daggers into her soul. Agatha's heart was pounding in her chest, and she might pass out, but she didn't care. The stress of a wedding and a crime scene was hard enough without family drama, even if she did bring it on herself.

"As much as I appreciate a *Jerry Springer* interlude," Coil said, "let's focus our attention on the victim."

Now it was Hank's turn to rub her back soothingly and try to bring her temper down to a simmer.

"I think the best thing is for you five to head back to the house and let us do our jobs," Hank said. "I know y'all are trying to help, but this is real life, and there's a dead man in there that Coil and Agatha both knew personally."

"I guess we know when we're not wanted," Brenda said. "You always do pick women over your family."

"Yes," Hank said. "I will always pick my wife over my family, because the second we say *I do* she becomes my family. I will always love you. But these terror tactics are going to stop."

"The Uber driver will be here in a minute," Gayle said. "We can wait outside until he gets here, and then I don't know about the rest of you but I'm packing my bags."

Gayle grabbed Brenda's hand and they stormed out the front door.

"Don't worry about them," Betty said, giving an apologetic smile. "They've always been the hotheaded ones. They'll come to their senses soon."

Hazel hadn't said a word, but she was still staring at Agatha like she was trying to decide whether or not to pull the grenade pin.

"You'll do," Hazel finally said with a nod. "Hank needs someone he can't steamroll just as much as he needs someone who will defend him, even from his own family." She nodded again and then followed Betty and Patsy out the door to wait with the others.

Agatha blew out a breath when they were gone. "I'm sorry, honey," she said, wrapping her arm around Hank.

"It's okay," he said. "We can't control other people's actions. The ball is in their court." Then he looked at Coil. "Sorry for the family drama."

Coil snorted. "You think this is family drama? Shelly's sister cheated on her husband with his twin, and I had to arrest our own niece for pooping in the neighbor's pool because they played their music too loud. We can't pick our blood. We can only put up boundaries to deflect the fallout."

"Wise words," Agatha said. "If y'all don't mind, I'd love to put all my energy into finding who killed Brad."

"Amen, sister," Coil said.

"So I'm guessing the working theory is that the hearse, the body, and Brad's murder are all related."

"Seems like a safe bet," Coil said. "We'll run the plate numbers on Brad's fleet of hearses and see if any are missing. I'm going to go with my gut on this one and start treating this as if Brad was using the funeral home for nefarious purposes."

"What nefarious purposes?" she asked.

"Who knows," Coil said. "Whoever those mercenaries work for approached Brad with a proposition he couldn't refuse. And knowing Brad like I do, he probably ticked off the money man by either not paying his debts or just being a jerk in general. He had a tendency toward both."

"What now?" Agatha asked.

"We've got blood and ballistics to process," Hank said. "And we need to get the autopsy results sooner rather than later. I want to know what was being transported in that body."

"What would you guess is in him?" she asked.

"Drugs or money," Coil said. "The usual bad-guy stuff."

"Maybe," Hank said. "But mercenaries are usually ex-military." He paced back and forth with his hands on his hips and his head down. His heart was pounding and his skin was clammy. Why hadn't he thought of it sooner? He'd let his sisters distract him, but that was no excuse when lives were on the line.

"Hank, what is it?" Agatha asked. "What's wrong?"

What if it's something more dangerous?" Hank asked.

"Like what?" Coil asked.

"Think big and bad," Hank said. "What can do the most damage?"

Coil's brows went up in surprise. "You're thinking the body might be a bomb?"

"I've seen it before," Hank said. "We need to get the bomb squad in and see if we can get x-rays before they open him up."

Coil was already on the radio making the request. "I sent James to the morgue," he said, looking at Hank with panic in his eyes.

"Just get them out," Hank said calmly. "Get everyone out of the building, until we can secure it."

"I'll call James," Agatha said.

An alert went off on all their phones and they read the incoming message from the command center.

"Oh God," Coil said, dropping down into a chair. "We're too late."

Agatha read the message for the fourth time, and tears came to her eyes. *Explosion at Bell County Morgue. Fire and Rescue on scene. Containing the fire before searching for survivors.*

"Maybe he hadn't gotten there yet," Agatha said. "Maybe he stopped to get something to eat after we left from the highway."

"I'll check." Coil's voice was empty and hollow, and he turned away as he made a call into dispatch to get information.

When he turned back to face them Agatha could see the answer in his eyes. "James's patrol car was parked out front. He was there."

"This is my fault," Hank said. "I'm sorry. I've seen this before. I should've made sure that body was handled with more care."

"How were you supposed to know that?" Agatha asked. "Your sisters ran over him and dumped him on our lawn for Pete's sake. This is not your fault. Or anyone's fault."

Coil nodded. "I need to call the Rangers in on this. We're going to need as many hands as we can get."

"Good," Agatha said. "We'll all help however we can. This is personal. Someone needs to call Karl and let him know. He and Heather were supposed to head out on vacation, but I don't want him to hear it from the news."

"Word like this spreads fast through the department," Coil said. "I guarantee he already knows."

"We can't get in over at the morgue until the fire department deals with the fire," Hank said. "But we can work this scene here and see if we find anything to lead us to those men. We owe it to James and whoever else was in that building to bring them justice."

CHAPTER FIVE

Several hours later, Hank milled around the sheriff's office waiting for Karl.

Coil had been in his office dealing with the media, the Texas Rangers, and whoever was in charge of the Austin FBI field office. The feebs got a little hinky when foreign mercenaries started shooting things up. He also knew that Coil was experienced in dealing with the bureaucracy of territorial policing. Which was why Hank was glad Coil was the sheriff instead of him.

He heard the beeps of the keypad that allowed employees into the back entrance, and he turned to see Rodriguez coming through the door. Her uniform was wilted and dirty, and he knew she'd been on the scene of the explosion. Her face was blotchy from crying.

He looked around and noticed the sheriff's office was more crowded than usual. Bell County had several sheriff's offices in the different towns that made up the county, but the one in Rusty Gun was the main office. The department was big, and stretched a lot of miles, and there were officers inside he'd never seen before. It hit him then that this was probably the first time most of them had lost one of their own. He'd spent his career working in the big city on big cases, and he'd lost more friends in the line of duty than he cared to count.

Crime in Bell County was relatively low. They were used to dealing with escaped cows or traffic accidents for the most part. He watched Agatha go to Rodriguez and throw her arms around her, and the two women wept openly.

He saw Coil hang up the phone and put his head in his hands, so he went to the office and knocked on the door. Coil waved him in.

"Any news?"

"The special agent in charge at the FBI is upset because we didn't notify him first. He mentioned something about reopening the ethics violation against me, and then I might have mentioned how I heard the FBI was doing an internal investigation on his house because of dirty practices. The conversation went downhill from there."

Hank grinned. "Are they going to assist with forensics, or actually send agents out to help?"

"He wouldn't commit. For the time being, the state crime lab is examining the blood and the bullet. Will Ellis called earlier to say that their Ranger crime scene techs had finished up processing Brad Hartley's murder. Will said they did find one bullet casing and it matches the one we recovered off the highway."

"Any luck with the hospitals?" Hank asked. "No way could that guy Hazel hit with her .44 not need emergency medical attention."

"We called the hospitals in Bell County, but no GSWs have been admitted. If they are mercenaries, the unlucky one probably got dumped off a bridge. It's not like there's much honor among thieves."

"Good point," Hank said. "I wonder if they knew the body was rigged with explosives?"

"Probably," Coil said. "But I'm still not sure if they're cartel or government contractors. That might also explain why they took off on the highway instead of pressing the fight to recover the corpse. I bet they were expecting it to detonate once Hazel parked on top of the thing."

Hank blew out a breath. "Things could've ended very badly. I think God was watching out for my sisters today."

"I don't know what to do about James," Coil admitted. "I don't know how to deal with all the hurting people out there. Because I'm hurting too."

"This is a tough one," Hank said. "But those cops out there are going to look to you for guidance. Don't be afraid to show them that you're human."

"You're right," he said. "But I'm so angry."

"Look on the bright side," Hank said. "Maybe you'll get to take it out on a mercenary."

"Fingers crossed," he said. "Let's go get the team focused on bringing these guys in."

People were crammed into the conference room and spilled out into the hallway. Somber expressions greeted them. Hank knew how important it was for the leader to show strength, but most importantly humanity, in times of crisis.

"It's been a tough day," Coil said. "And I know we've all been waiting for confirmation about Deputy James, so I won't beat around the bush. It's been confirmed that James, as well as the medical examiner and an, as of yet, unidentified victim, were all killed in the explosion today.

"We have five eyewitnesses who can give a decent

description of what the suspects look like. We're also waiting for an expedited forensics processing on the bullet casings from the funeral home and collected off the highway. Those along with the blood sample aren't expected to tell us much, but we're hopeful. Hank has had experience dealing with mercenaries for hire before using these kinds of tactics, so he's going to distribute assignments."

Hank nodded and moved to the front of the room. "I want paired patrols canvassing neighborhoods and business districts. I want to know if these guys are in our county or across county lines. This is our priority. If someone is egregiously breaking the law, then take care of it, but lay off on the speeding tickets tonight until this is closed up. I'm going to assign two units to take care of calls from dispatch, and we'll adjust as needed. Everyone else, I want out on the streets.

"Springer, I want you to start running the financials on Brad Hartley and the Sweet Dreams Funeral Home. Brad's smuggling front is what brought these men here, so there has to be records of payments or cash transactions. You may find the sole thread tying us to a suspect."

"I'm on it," Springer said.

"Lieutenant Rodriguez, I need you on the phone with the state crime lab. Don't take no for an answer, and make sure they run the blood and ballistics through every database known to man. You're in charge of assigning calls coming in, and if you need to reassign patrol units that's up to you."

Rodriguez nodded.

"Karl, I want you to head out with the Rangers. There's a man with a GSW to the chest who probably didn't survive. Check rivers and under bridges, and keep an eye out for that hearse. They might have torched it or tried to bury it in the lake.

"Coil and I are going to meet with the witnesses again and see if we can pull any other information from them."

"What about me?" Agatha asked.

"I want you to research and record," Hank said. "This has been a fast and furious kind of day. I want a murder board set up in this office, and I need a timeline of events. The more time passes, the harder it is to remember times and who talked to who."

Agatha nodded, and Hank looked around the room as a whole. "Let's get this done. For James."

"For James," they repeated in unison.

***

Hank and Coil hadn't said much on the short ride over from the sheriff's office to Hank's home. He knew his sisters were hurt and mad, and it had been so many years he had no idea how to bridge the gap. Even more, he wasn't sure he wanted to. He'd learned over the years that toxic people sucked the joy out of life, and unless his sisters changed their attitude, they were toxic to his relationship with Agatha.

None of them had answered the phone when Hank had called, so they'd driven back to his house in hopes they'd be there and not driving back to Philadelphia.

"I don't mean to pry," Coil said, making Hank snort. "But what's up with your sisters? Why'd all the fighting start?"

"Family is messy and complicated," Hank said. "I can't

really pinpoint when things changed. I was the baby, and our parents died while I was still young, so I guess the girls felt an obligation to raise me. Can you imagine having five mothers? Five very different mothers who all combined knew exactly nothing about raising a young boy. None of them ever had kids of their own, but they've always had that manipulative spirit. They were smothering. Even when they got husbands of their own, they'd say things like they couldn't have their own children because they were too busy taking care of me. I couldn't wait to get out of that house."

"Major guilt trip," Coil said, whistling.

"It was always something like that. They made me feel like I was obligated to stay there and take care of them because that's what they'd done for me. They didn't want me to go off for college. I got a full scholarship, and you've have thought I'd shot someone in the head by the way they reacted. It got to the point where I just didn't tell them anything, and when it was time to leave for school I packed a bag and left. I got to listen to more of the same every time I came home for Christmas or Thanksgiving. And they were thrilled to cheer me on at graduation because they thought I'd be moving back home and getting a job in town. But I got accepted to the police academy. I got into the Philadelphia Police Academy after graduation, and then I was sent to training at Quantico and I was there for a year. And then things really started to go downhill.

"I'd get calls with requests to get them out of speeding tickets. Then it became a request for help with a DWI. Then there was a bar fight and unpaid tabs. It was embarrassing. And by that time I started to understand that while I was grateful they chose to raise me instead of sticking me in the foster system, I didn't owe them anything. And then Tammy and I got engaged."

"And I guess that didn't go over well?" Coil asked.

"Like a ton of bricks."

They turned onto Hank's street, but there was no minivan in the driveway.

"They hated Tammy," Hank said. "They saw her as a threat, and they never even tried to make her feel welcome. Just like how they're doing with Agatha. But how they treated Tammy was the last straw for me. That's when I cut all ties. I haven't seen them for another holiday or anything else since then. They didn't even come to her funeral. And then they started calling and inviting me to things again as if nothing had ever happened."

"Well," Coil said. "We need a plan B. Because your sisters aren't here, and I really need to talk to them."

"You know anyone at the phone company?" Hank asked.

"As a matter of fact, I do," Coil said. "Let me give them a call and see if we can track their cells."

CHAPTER SIX

Agatha stared at the newly created murder board and her timeline until her eyes crossed. Hank was right about the value of having a tight timeline of activities. Everything had happened so fast that the events of the morning seemed like a million years ago. It had only been hours since she'd talked to James out on the highway where the shoot-out had taken place between Hazel and one of the bandits. And now he was gone.

There was too much information swirling around in her head. Between the crime scene facts and the calls and confirmations she was getting about the wedding, a migraine was brewing.

The thought of canceling the wedding all together had crossed her mind.

"How's it going?" Springer asked.

"Slow," she said. "I've hit a wall."

"I know what you mean. Research is tedious, but there's always a treasure trove of hidden facts to be discovered if you just dig deep enough."

"I can relate. Research is second nature when I'm

writing a book. But sometimes you've just got to take a step back and let everything soak in. I think I'm going to take a walk or something. I need to clear my head."

"Sounds good," he said. "I'm still wading through the mess of Hartley's finances or I'd be right there with you."

"I understand," she said, closing her laptop. "I'm going to leave my stuff here. I won't be gone long."

She grabbed her bag and put on her old ball cap, pulling her ponytail through the hole in the back. The light blue, long-sleeve T-shirt she'd tied around her waist hung over her black yoga pants. She used the back door because the press were camped out in the front, and she didn't want to see anyone or talk to anyone asking questions about James.

She circled around and headed up Main Street, and then she cut back across to where she'd parked her Jeep.

"Agatha," Heather called out.

Agatha spun around and saw Heather standing in the doorway of the Kettle Café. She must've been having dinner or was waiting on Karl to take a break.

"You scared me," Agatha said, putting a hand over her racing heart.

"I figured you'd show up at some point with your Jeep parked right here." Heather came out of the restaurant on her sky-high heels and threw herself into Agatha's arms.

"Oh, honey," she said. "I'm so sorry. This is all a horrible nightmare."

"I still haven't wrapped my head around it," Agatha admitted. "It's been good to stay busy."

"Is there anything I can do? I hate feeling so helpless. Karl said he might get a few minutes to swing by and update me in the next hour or so, so I thought I'd just stay close."

"The best thing you can do is pray," Agatha said.

"We've got to stick together as a community through this and protect our own."

"I know you, Agatha Harley, and you can't lie and say you don't have your wedding on your mind too. And you feel guilty because you're thinking of that instead of putting all your attention on what happened to Deputy James."

Agatha's mouth dropped open. Sometimes Heather surprised her.

"Don't you dare think about cancelling that wedding," Heather scolded. "You've waited too long for your knight in shining armor, and life goes on."

"I'm not sure what to do about the wedding, but I know whatever it is, Hank will support me. Right now though, we have to solve this case."

"Agreed, girl," Heather said. "Y'all have any leads?"

Agatha shook her head. "But I want to see these guys leaving in the same hearse they rode in on. And not in the front seat, if you get my drift."

"I think the whole town is in agreement on that," Heather said. "You need to de-stress. You're getting those little lines between your brows. As soon as this is over I'm going to have my hair girl give you the works. My treat. She'll see me any time I want. Maybe you can finally start to feel like a bride."

"I'll let you know," Agatha said noncommittally. "I've got to go find that hearse so these guys can have a meeting with their maker."

"I saw a hearse earlier today behind the old meatpacking plant," Heather said. "You know the one toward Austin? I guess they probably have a lot of room in the back for hauling stuff."

Agatha had already checked out of the conversation, her attention on James's death and whether or not she should cancel the wedding." She waved bye to Heather and got in the Jeep. Taking a drive would clear her head, and then she could get back to work. She drove through the old part of town where she and Hank lived, and she noticed there were no cars parked in front of their house. Apparently, the interviews with the sisters were happening somewhere else. She cleared her mind and drove aimlessly.

And then she slammed her brakes on as Heather's last words finally penetrated. She did a U-turn in the middle of the road and headed back to town, coming to a screeching halt in front of the Kettle Café. Heather's little red convertible was still parked out front.

She hopped out and ran into the restaurant, cornering Heather in her usual table by the front window.

"What did you say earlier? Before I left."

"Huh?" Heather asked. "Have you been drinking? You look a mess."

"Just tell me what you said about the hearse."

"I said they must have lots of cargo space. I saw one outside the meatpacking plant."

"Are you sure you saw a hearse?"

"Positive," she said. "It sticks out like a sore thumb. I was coming back from Austin and got detoured because of construction on Interstate 35. Then I ended up on some side road in the middle of nowhere and I didn't have any cell service, so my GPS wasn't working. All I could do was keep driving. I got a real good view, because you come up on this hill and you can look down over the whole thing. That's when I saw the black hearse sitting around back."

"Thanks," Agatha said. "You've been a big help."

She ran back out to her Jeep without saying goodbye this time, and she tried to get Hank on the phone. There was no answer. She called Coil and got the same result.

"Come on, guys," she said, speeding toward the highway.

She knew exactly where Heather was talking about. That old meatpacking plant was a hundred years old, and it was a real eyesore. She kept hearing whispers about someone like Chip and Joanna coming in to turn it into some store or park, but so far, it had just been rumor.

She kept calling Hank and Coil, but had no luck and she hit her palm on the steering wheel in frustration. She got off the highway and stayed on the access road, following the twists and turns that led to the top of the hill. There was still just enough daylight to see the meatpacking plant.

She stopped the car and got out. The plant was huge and industrial with smokestacks and areas gated off by chain-link fence. But sure enough, there was a black hearse parked off to the side closest to the bone yard along with a white van. The bone yard was where they'd dumped bones and undesirable parts of the carcass when the plant had been in operation. She remembered the black smoke that had billowed into the sky and the scary stories told about the bone yard. It was still full of bones and gravel and rocks.

Agatha took out her phone one more time and tried to call Hank and Coil, but Heather had been right. Reception wasn't good out here. She sent a text and crossed her fingers it went through. All she needed to do was confirm that this was the same hearse that Hank's sisters had come across that morning. Once she did, she could go back for reinforcements.

With her mind made up, she moved her Jeep off to the shoulder under some trees and set off on foot.

There were broken windows all across the front, and the chain-link fence was cut and rusted. There was thick tree cover on the south side, so she decided to stick toward the overgrown bushes and vines that had woven themselves into the fencing. That was probably all it had holding it up. Her favorite yoga pants did nothing to stop the briars from ripping across her thighs. She found a gap in the fence big enough for her to crawl through, and she looked around to make sure no one had seen her.

She was leaving the cover of the trees and going into an open, graveled area that was almost the size of a football field. To her back were the trees, to her right was a steep drop-off that led to the bone yard, and directly in front and to her left was the plant.

The incline was somewhat steep, so she tried to stay low to the ground and scoot down until she was on level ground. The dust from the gravel kicked up around her and got in her eyes, and she bit back a cry as the palm of her hand was cut on a sharp rock.

She was doing this for Deputy James. The sooner she discovered whether or not the hearse was the one in question, the sooner his killers could be brought to justice.

"You can do this, Agatha. No big deal. Check out the hearse, and then get out of Dodge."

She wiped her bloody hand on her leggings, took a deep breath, and sprinted full out until she skidded into the side of the hearse. It was louder than she thought it would be and she ducked low by the tire to catch her breath.

Her eyes burned and she blinked rapidly to clear the dust, and she held her breath as she listened for footsteps or any other signs of life. She looked under the hearse, but there was nothing to see from that angle.

Once her heartbeat slowed and her eyes stopped watering, her other senses took over. The smell was horrendous, and she gagged slightly and clamped a hand over her mouth. She got back low to the ground and hoped the air was fresher down there. It wasn't.

When she heard the buzzing in her ears she thought it was a sign that she was about to pass out, but then she saw them hovering around the vehicle like a cloud. Once her mind had time to clear, she understood the ramifications of the stench and blowflies. Death wasn't unfamiliar to her.

All she had to do was pop up and look inside the hearse. She was willing to bet the stench belonged to the guy Hazel had shot.

Agatha tried to spring to her feet but was surprised at how sluggish her legs were. The low crawl and Texas heat had zapped her energy. She stumbled sideways before catching her balance, and she pressed both hands against the back window and looked through the tinted glass. She held her breath as best she could, and pressed her face against the window.

There he was. Flies covered him and his white shirt was soaked with dried blood that had turned black. He looked just as Hazel had described him—dark hair, black suit with a white shirt and black tie.

With this guy dead, that meant there were three left. Even as she had the thought, glass shattered above her head, and the sound of a rifle being fired reverberated off the concrete building.

She dropped back down to her knees, her breath labored and sweat streaming into her eyes. Her only thought was survival, and her only way out was back toward the fence where she'd come. She was a sitting duck if she stayed where she was, and her only chance was to run and pray.

She took a deep breath and launched herself toward the fence line as bullets ricocheted around her.

CHAPTER SEVEN

Hank had to admit he was relieved his sisters had checked into the resort where he and Agatha planned to hold their reception instead of hightailing it back to Philly. It was fortunate Coil was friends with the owner. It made it much easier to deal with police matters, especially after their last investigation when a celebrity chef was murdered right on the property.

"Oh, Mr. Davidson," the manager said, scurrying over. "So nice to see you again, and we're certainly looking forward to your reception in a couple of weeks. Your sisters checked in today, and they insisted on the Alamo Suite, which isn't part of your room block for the wedding. I went ahead and bumped them up for you, but I told them that particular room is reserved for several days next week, so we'll need to move them back to a regular room. I know they're upset, but it's completely out of our control."

Hank sighed. "I'm sure you did more than you had to," he said kindly. "And I appreciate you upgrading them. Please put the charges on my tab. I'll take care of it."

"Oh, no, Mr. Davidson," the manager said. "Mr. Swan

insisted that he take care of any bills you might incur for the wedding. It's our pleasure after everything you did for us."

"I appreciate that," Hank said, already feeling the guilt creep in. "But don't let them take advantage of you or the staff. If they think it's a free ticket, everybody here will hate to see me coming."

The manager smiled. "Will do, Mr. Davidson."

"What floor is the Alamo Suite on?" Hank asked.

"Top floor," he said. "There are only suites up there, so you'll need a key card to access the elevator. Let me get you one."

Hank and Coil thanked the manager again and headed up to the top floor. His sisters weren't going to be happy to see him, but he didn't much care.

"If we're going to get anything out of them, you're going to have to handle this," Hank said. "We don't do anything but rub each other the wrong way."

"I'm done playing games," Coil said. "If they don't cooperate things are going to get unpleasant."

Coil knocked on the door of the Alamo Suite and waited for someone to answer the door. Hank could feel eyes on them on the other side of the peephole. The door opened a crack, but the deadbolt was on. Gayle stood on the other side. Of all his sisters, she was the most ornery.

"What do y'all want?" she asked.

"I need to ask you all some more questions, and I need to collect Hazel's gun. I should have done it earlier, but things got hectic."

"You hear that, Hazel," she called back over her shoulder. "They're here to take your gun."

"Over my dead body," Hazel called back from the other room.

"You heard her," Gayle said, shrugging, and she tried to shut the door, but Coil's foot kept it from closing.

"I wasn't making a request," Coil said. "I will speak with each of you and I will take that gun. We can do it the easy way or the hard way. It's up to you. I suggest you let me in, and we can do this in the comfort of your own room."

Gayle narrowed her eyes at Coil, and then she turned her glare on Hank. "This is your doing, isn't it? You think to get back at us, so you have your cop buddies roust us?"

Hank was grinding his teeth so hard he was surprised they hadn't turned to dust, but he stayed quiet and let Coil take the lead.

"Come on in, I guess," Gayle said. "We've already told you everything we know."

"You never know," Coil said, following her into a ridiculously large room where the five sisters had been watching a marathon of *The Bachelor*.

Hank took a seat in a hard wooden dining chair out of the way, and pulled his phone out of his pocket. He put it on the table and then sat back to observe.

"Do you want something to drink?" Betty asked, coming up to him and whispering like she might get in trouble if the others found out she was being hospitable.

"Water if you have it," Hank said. "Thanks, Betty."

She smiled dreamily and went to get a couple of waters from the stocked refrigerator in the kitchen.

"I don't know if you've heard," Hank said, "but there was an explosion at the morgue earlier today. Right after we parted company at the funeral home, as a matter of fact."

"You blaming us for something?" Patsy asked. "'Cause I'll call our lawyer if we need to."

"I'm not blaming you," he said. "I'm trying to tell you how lucky you are to be alive. The bomb was inside the body you rolled over and then transported into Rusty Gun. It could've gone off at any time."

Five identical looks of shock came over their faces, and then they all started talking at once. Hank took his water and stood. He was too restless to sit still.

Betty came up beside him again. "Is that true?" she asked.

He nodded, and she burst into tears before throwing her arms around him. It took him by surprise. He couldn't remember the last time he'd hugged one of his sisters.

"We've got three dead for sure," Coil said, "including one of my officers."

"Oh, no," Patsy said, placing her hand over her heart. "End of watch. Rest in peace, brother."

"I need details," Coil said. "Do any of you remember a partial license plate? Were they all carrying the same kind of gun? Had you noticed them on the road before? Maybe at a gas station or a stop light. Did any of them look familiar? How old do you think they were?"

"Okay, okay," Hazel said. "We get the point."

They asked questions and tried to jog their memories for almost two hours, but they got very little new information. All they knew for certain was they were white males between the ages of twenty-five and thirty-five, which also fit in with the profile of them being ex-military.

Coil blew out a breath and he and Hank shared a look. "Okay, ladies," Coil said. "We appreciate your help." Then he looked at Hazel. "I still need the gun so we can run ballistics in case a body turns up. Is it registered?"

"Of course it's registered," she said. "My husband gave me that gun for our twentieth anniversary. It wasn't so heavy back then."

Hank heard a phone buzzing and looked around to see

where it was coming from. He'd completely forgotten he'd left his phone on the table, and the call was coming for him. He picked it up and saw Springer's name on the screen, as well as several missed calls from Agatha. He furrowed his brow and answered the phone.

"Springer," Hank said. "What's going on?"

"I got a hit on the financials," he said. "It looks like the bank had started foreclosure proceedings against the funeral home about three years ago. That's when Brad took over after his father died."

"Was it failing before?"

"Nope. It was flush with cash, but once Brad got his hands on it, the place fell apart. He had plenty of business, but he has a spending problem. Then about a year ago he started getting an influx of extra income."

"Can you tell where it's coming from?"

"I did some digging, and the ACH deposits led me to a children's non-profit. Of course, after doing a little digging it turns out it's not real. I'm still digging, but the deeper I go the more walls I hit. I'm going to need search warrants, but they're going to fight us on them. Big companies don't like people poking into their business."

"You're right. Big companies don't give up client data without a fight. Especially corrupt ones," Hank said.

"Y'all coming back to the office?"

"Probably so. Coil is wrapping things up now, and it'll be dark soon," Hank replied. "Is Agatha nearby? I saw she tried to call."

"Oh, I thought she might be with you. She took a break about an hour ago and never came back. She's made good progress on the board. She just needed to clear her head. But I really thought she'd be back by now. Reports are piling up on her laptop."

"She's not here with us," Hank said, the urge to call Agatha overwhelming. "Good work, Springer." And then he disconnected and called Agatha back. It went straight to voicemail.

"Agatha called," Coil said, holding up his phone.

"Yeah, I know," Hank said.

Coil looked at Hank worriedly. "You think something is wrong?"

"Springer said she left for a break an hour ago and hasn't come back. I'm sure she had to do something for the wedding. But her phone is going directly to voicemail."

"She tried calling me several times," Coil said. "I had it turned down so I could get through with your sisters. I didn't realize we'd been going for so long."

"Me either," Hank said, scrolling back through his texts. Sure enough, Agatha had left him a message.

Hearse. 1001 Bison Road.

"Oh, no," Hank said.

"What's wrong?"

"What's at 1001 Bison Road?"

Coil typed it into his GPS. "Looks like the old meat-packing plant. Why?"

"Looks like Agatha found a hearse."

"Surely she wouldn't go there by herself," Coil said.

"She would if she felt time was of the essence and no one answered her calls, but I don't think she'd put herself in danger. For all I know she saw it on her way to do wedding stuff and was just calling it in. Her phone is either dead or turned off. Either way, I need to track her down."

"Come on," Coil said. "I'll call in a team."

"No, your guys are stretched thin as it is. I don't want to take them away from their assignments until we have proof. Just drop me at my car, and I'll do a drive-by and see if I can confirm a hearse. It'll be dark soon, so I need to get moving. I'll keep you on speed dial just in case."

Coil shook his head. "If you say so, buddy. But if you find that hearse, I want to get a team out there before you decide to be a hero."

"Hey, I am a hero," Hank said, trying to lighten the mood. "Agatha tells me I'm her hero all the time."

Hank had parked his car at the opposite end of the block from the sheriff's office to avoid getting trapped in, and he bid Coil farewell as he hopped out of the pickup truck and went to his Beemer. He plugged the address into his GPS and headed toward the highway.

The GPS seemed confused by the roads and construction, and he ended up on an access road that wound like a snake up to the top of a hill. He had no idea if he was going the right direction.

His phone rang, and his heart jumped at the possibility it might be Agatha, but it was Heather's name that came across the screen.

"What's up, Heather?" he asked. "I can't talk long."

"I was trying to get hold of Agatha," she said. "Her phone is going directly to voicemail, but I need to get in touch with her. I managed to get us scheduled for the works tomorrow at my salon."

"I'm looking for her now," he said. "She sent me a text to look at something out on Bison Road."

"Oh, that's the old meatpacking plant," Heather said. "I told her I saw a hearse out there earlier today, and she took off like a chicken with her head cut off."

"You're saying Agatha was heading out to find the hearse?"

"Yep," she said.

"How long ago was that?" Hank asked.

"I don't know. A couple hours maybe."

Hank hung up the phone and pressed the gas a little harder, and then he slammed on the brakes when he got to the top of the hill. There was Agatha's Jeep parked on the side of the road, and Agatha was nowhere to be found. And directly below him outside the meatpacking plant was the hearse every cop in the entire county had been looking for.

He dialed Coil and waited for him to pick up. "I need a team," Hank said as soon as Coil answered. "I think Aggie's in trouble. The hearse is here, and Agatha's Jeep is here, but I don't see her anywhere."

"I'll see what units are in the area and get a team together," Coil said. "I'm on my way now. Stay put until we get there."

Hank gave a vague *hmm* so he didn't have to lie to his friend, and they disconnected. He backed up and pulled to the side of the road so he could park behind Agatha, and then he got out and started looking for anything that would lead him to her.

From the top of the hill he could still see the highway, but he realized how secluded the area around the plant really was. There were no homes or businesses. Just wide-open land and what looked like a quarry off to the side of the plant. He got his binoculars out of the trunk and got a closer look. Not a quarry. It looked like...bones.

He scanned the area around the hearse, but it was getting too dark to see anything of consequence. He was going to have to look with his own eyes. He tossed the binoculars back in the car and made sure his phone was on silent. He didn't have a bulletproof vest or anything for protection. Only the weapon at his side.

Before he made the trek down the hill, he searched inside Agatha's Jeep with his flashlight. No phone, and no signs of struggle or blood that he could see. Agatha was smart. She was alive and well. He had to believe that.

Hank stayed to the tree cover as he made his way down the hill to an old chain-link fence that was overgrown with vines and shrubs. There was just enough light left so he could see one foot in front of the other, but if he delayed he was going to be stuck in complete darkness with no sense of direction.

There had to be an opening in the fence somewhere. There weren't easily accessible options for entry inside the gated area unless someone drove directly to the front of the plant. He was sure this was the way Agatha would've taken.

He moved vines and branches, searching for a tear in the fence large enough for him to fit through. But then he saw the opening a few yards down. That was it. There was no place else she could've gone through.

The rusted chain link caught on his shirt and pants as he tried to slip through, and the fabric tore as he muscled his way out of the tangled web. Agatha was quite a bit smaller than he was, so she'd probably slipped through with no problems. His shoe crunched down on something solid, and what sounded like glass cracking had him lifting his foot gently.

He crouched down and felt along the ground until his fingers touched a cell phone. He recognized the case. It was Agatha's. His heart started pounding a little harder, and he looked around, praying she'd be right there.

His vision was slowly acclimating to the darkness, and he could clearly see the expanse of open incline that led down to the hearse. His cell phone was buzzing in his pocket and he knew it was Coil.

Fury enveloped him at the thought of Agatha putting herself in danger. What had she been thinking?

The darkness played to his advantage, and as long as the moon stayed behind the clouds he had a shot at making it across the long expanse of loose rocks without being seen. Hank stayed low and shuffled down the incline, sliding on rocks and skinning his hands and knees in the process. He was soaked in sweat, and the closer he got to the hearse the worse the smell became.

He was in the final stretch of his destination and he paused long enough to grab his weapon and catch his breath. He'd never been so glad he'd been keeping up his workouts at the gym. Every muscle in his body was aching.

Hank moved in a low-crouched position toward the hearse, and stifled a grunt when something tangled around his legs and caused him to fall forward on his hands. He kept hold of his weapon, but his other hand took the brunt of the fall, and he knew the skin was shredded from the rocks.

He stayed motionless, listening for sounds that indicated his cover had been blown, and then he untangled the garment from around his feet. It was a long-sleeved shirt—one he recognized belonging to Agatha.

He looked from the shirt to the hearse and inhaled the smell of death, and then he prayed like he'd never prayed before that he wasn't about to find Agatha dead.

He made himself move, flinging himself toward the hearse and skidding to a halt by the back tire. The smell made his eyes water, and flies buzzed around him, agitated he'd disturbed their scavenging.

He took out a small penlight from his pocket and cupped his hand around it, sticking it through the broken window so he could see inside the hearse. Then he let out a sigh of relief when he realized it wasn't Agatha, but the man Hazel had shot.

His cell phone buzzed again in his pocket and he looked around the wide-open space and then back toward the cover of trees and the jagged drop-off that led to the bone yard. Agatha was still out there somewhere. She could be injured. He had to find her.

His best bet was to go back to the tree cover. That was the smartest place to hide until she could make it back to her car. He took a step forward and the bullet smashed through the window of the hearse, exactly where he'd just been standing. There was no time to think or panic. He ran with everything he had left, zigzagging his way back up the rocky incline as bullets continued to ping around him.

CHAPTER EIGHT

Agatha jerked at the sounds of gunshots, and she hunkered into a ball behind the shrubs she'd found for cover. She heard the rushing footfalls and hoped she didn't get tripped over. She'd been able to elude the killers since that first shot almost claimed her life.

Her muscles had cramped up from staying still so long, and she didn't know how quickly she could move if she had to. Had she been there minutes or hours or days? She had no idea. All she knew was that she was alone, and Hank would eventually come to look for her. She'd sent him the address, and potentially lured him directly to the killers.

Her breath caught in her chest at the thought and panic overwhelmed her. Her mind felt slow and sluggish. The killers were shooting at someone. Someone who shouldn't have been there. It had to be Hank. She had to believe that or she might lose her mind. And he had to be okay.

She didn't know where she was. Running back up the rocky hill had been more of a challenge than coming down, and she'd slipped off the edge of the ravine into the bone yard, the sharp fragments cutting into her like little knives.

She knew she was bleeding and hurt, but she didn't know how bad.

Adrenaline and survival mode had kicked in and she crawled her way out of the ravine and back into the trees, and then she'd kept going until she'd found a rocky ledge overgrown with bushes where she could hide. They'd come to look for her. She'd heard their footsteps and their shouts to each other in a foreign tongue. But as the sun had gone down they'd retreated back into the plant.

The footsteps were getting closer and she could hear murmured voices as they canvassed the area, and she held her breath as leaves and twigs snapped beneath heavy footsteps. There was a grunt of pain as branches rustled on top of the ledge where she was hiding, and then a loud thump as a body fell over and landed on the ground only a few feet from her.

She was frozen in her spot—afraid to move—afraid the enemy was within arm's reach. Staying still and hidden was the best course of action. She could decide what to do in the morning when daylight came.

That might be easier said than done. She was freezing, and her teeth had started to chatter as the adrenaline had faded. And she was afraid she might have cracked a couple of ribs when she'd taken that fall because it hurt to breathe in too deeply, and the pain in her side was like nothing she'd ever felt before.

She could hear someone's labored breathing, and she synced her own breathing to his. She sensed his pain, but she didn't know if he was a good guy or a bad guy and she couldn't risk it. There was rustling where the man lay and a couple of grunts. She turned her head slowly, trying to peep between the branches she'd moved to hide her spot, and she saw the faint glow of light.

Then she heard the sweetest sound she could've asked for.

"Coil," Hank said. "Pick up, buddy. Where's that backup? I'm hurt pretty bad. Be careful coming in. They're armed with assault rifles."

She pushed the branches aside. "Hank," she whispered. "It's me."

"Aggie?" Hank asked.

A sob escaped before she could help it and she nodded furiously before she remembered he couldn't see anything in the dark. "It's me," she said. "Are you okay?"

"It's my back," he said.

"You're not shot?"

"Not yet," he said. "Just scrapes and cuts and a busted back. What about you? Are you hurt?"

"Same," she said. "I might have a couple of broken ribs, but I can run if we have to."

"That makes one of us," he said.

She heard the rustle of branches. "What are you doing? Let me help you."

"No, stay where you are," he said. "Whatever your cover is, it's good. I can hear your voice, but I have no idea where you're hiding. I just need to maneuver myself out of this clearing. They're sweeping the area in a grid pattern. They'll get to us eventually. We just need to stay put until backup gets here."

"But you're hurt," she said. "I'm not going to let you sit out there and be the sacrificial lamb."

"I'll be fine," he said. "We'll both be dead if you break cover for me."

"I know one is dead for sure, so that leaves three of them," she said.

"I saw the body in the hearse," Hank whispered.

"Hank, I'm literally right above you in a little cavern under the ledge. We could touch hands if you stretched. Are you sure you don't want me to come to you?"

Hank didn't answer.

"Hank?" she whispered.

"Don't move," a man said from above.

He stood directly above her on the edge of the ledge, and it was obvious he'd either seen or heard Hank, she wasn't sure which. She could barely make out Hank's outline, and she wondered how well the man could see. Hank must have wondered too because she saw his arm move ever so slowly toward her and he placed his gun just where she could reach it.

She swallowed hard. She was more than comfortable with firearms, but things could go very wrong, very fast. Her hand crept forward and she wrapped it around the butt of the gun, and then she lay still and prayed she'd be able to lift it when the time came. Her arm was shaking like a leaf.

"I said, don't move," the man repeated.

"I don't suppose we can talk this out like gentlemen," Hank said. "I was just checking out the property for a potential investment. I didn't realize someone else had a bid in."

The man spoke impeccable English, but she had no visual of him. She needed him to come down where Hank was lying.

"Get up slowly," the man said. "We might as well shoot you inside the car with Martin. We'll set it on fire and be on our way."

"That sounds like an amazing plan," Hank said dryly. "But I'm going to need some help getting to my feet. I threw my back out when I fell and I can't move."

"Yeah, right," the man said, hopping off the ledge and coming down to where Hank lay sprawled on the ground.

Agatha could see his legs but not much else.

"What are y'all doing here?" Hank asked. "Hiding out? I have to say it's probably not a very good hiding spot. Especially with the dead guy in the car."

"We're not hiding from anything," he said. "We're just waiting for a ride. And I think it's a very good hiding spot. Other than another nosy real estate investor like you, we haven't seen a soul. I hate to shoot a man while he's down."

"Yeah, I'm real sorry about that," Hank said. "But like I said, I can't move anywhere. I can't even feel my legs. But I'd expect a coward to shoot an unarmed man while he's lying on the ground helpless."

"Coward?" the man asked. "I've served my country longer than you've been lying about being something you're not. I can smell cops a mile away. And I'm no coward."

Military? The profile had been right about that. Agatha knew Hank had struck a nerve in calling the man a coward. She also knew he was trying to get him in a position where she'd have a straight shot.

"Military?" Hank asked. "You didn't serve my country, I can tell you that for sure. Did you kill that man in the car back there?"

"Casualty of war."

"Word on the street is he got gunned down by an old lady."

"So you are a cop," the man said. "How many of you are here?"

"The whole place is surrounded. You guys aren't getting out of here."

"Then I've got nothing to lose," the man said.

Agatha felt the tension in the air skyrocket, and she

tightened her grasp on the gun. She held her breath, scared to exhale in case she was heard.

Before she realized what was happened the man's foot drew back and he kicked Hank in the ribs, causing Hank to cry out. She knew she'd made a noise, but hoped it had been covered by Hank's yell.

She watched in slow motion as the man raised his rifle, and it was all the warning she needed. She lifted the gun and fired, the kick doing something weird to her shoulder since she was holding it one-handed and at an odd angle. But she didn't have time to worry over it. She'd only hit the man in the thigh, which was enough to bring him to his knees and make him mad.

She rolled out of her protective covering and came to her knees. Her legs were too weak to stand, and she pointed the gun at him again, this time center mass, and she took the shot.

It echoed across the clearing, and the man slumped down onto the ground next to Hank.

"Nice job, ace," Hank said.

Her arms were so heavy she couldn't hold on to the gun anymore and it dropped to the ground. A sob caught in her throat, and she threw herself at Hank before she remembered her ribs, and then she was crying for a different reason.

"I don't mean to make light of the situation," Hank said. "But the two of us aren't doing so hot right now. I can't even imagine what our wedding night is going to be like. We're going to have to get creative."

Agatha hiccuped out a laugh.

"Hand me the gun," Hank said. "We've got two more coming for us, and we've just told them exactly where we are."

CHAPTER NINE

Hank hadn't been kidding when he'd told his attacker that he couldn't feel his legs. They were like dead weight. Now with the extra kick the guy had given him he had a couple of broken ribs to worry about too.

He needed to make sure Agatha was protected. He pulled an extra magazine from his pocket and went ahead and changed it out with the one she'd just fired from. Two extra bullets could mean the difference between life and death. He hit the automatic release button, and the empty magazine dropped from the gun's receiver into his hand. Then he used his forefinger to line up the loaded magazine and slid it into the weapon before racking the slide back to chamber a bullet ready to fire.

He'd practiced that maneuver for over twenty-six years and counting. He could reload a weapon in his sleep, and also through his pain. That wasn't the challenge. Taking the rifle off the dead man was going to be tough for someone who could only move from the waist up.

"Tell me what you need me to do," she said.

"If you could get my legs to work that would be a good start."

"You were serious about that?" she asked, the horror in her voice audible. "Oh God, Hank."

"Get the rifle from our friend here," he said. "And if you can stomach it, check his pockets for extra ammo."

"I can stomach it. He's not my first dead guy."

Agatha went about the task of collecting the gun and ammunition, and he tried to take stock of their position. It wasn't a terrible place to take cover. If Agatha could go back into her hidey-hole, and he could find cover behind some trees, they might have a chance. The men would have to come over the top of that ledge just like the last guy did. And with the moon out from the cloud cover now, that gave him perfect sight to see them coming.

"This might not be the best timing, but I want you to know I love you," she said.

"I love you too," he said. "And I'm sorry for this. These situations aren't what I was expecting during my retirement. I'm thinking we might need to make some changes after we get married."

"Oh, yeah?" Agatha asked. "Like a real retirement kind of change?"

"Something like that," he said. "It might be nice to buy some land. Build a house of our own. Maybe have some chickens and a garden."

He could see her grin in the dark. "Farmer Davidson," she said. "I guess that's the good thing about being able to work from anywhere. I can write and watch you wrangle chickens. I'm intrigued by the proposition."

At that moment, Hank couldn't have loved her more. She was solid as a rock, checking the pockets of the man

LILIANA HART & LOUIS SCOTT

she'd had to kill to save him, and she had a smile on her face trying to ease his worry.

"Found another pistol," she said, holding it up. "And an extra mag. And he's got an earpiece for communication."

"I need help getting behind some cover," he said. "If you could pull me from under my arms I can help as best I can."

She helped him into a sitting position, and he almost blacked out from the pain. Nausea roiled in his stomach and he dropped his head down and tried to take in some deep breaths.

"You can do it," Agatha said. "Just a little more."

Tears seeped from the corner of his eyes and quietly traced their way down his cheeks. Hank was no softie. He'd known pain and was lucky to have survived some of his battles while fighting the world's most dangerous serial killers, but he was helpless without the use of his legs.

"I need to be in a spot where I can pick them off as they come over the ledge, but I don't think I can't do this," he said. "I can barely sit up, and I'm not even sure I can hold my arm up to fire a weapon."

"Then let me do it for you," she said. "I can be your legs and your trigger finger. Just tell me what to do."

Agatha was an amazing woman. She was brilliant and street smart and she thought like a cop. But she didn't have the years of experience in the field like he did. She could handle a weapon, but she didn't know evasion tactics, or how to move like a ghost. And she wouldn't be able to overpower these men in hand-to-hand combat. They were military. They were trained. And it was asking too much of her.

"Go find a safe place to hide," he said. "Coil will be here with reinforcements soon. You take the rifle and you can lay down cover if I get in trouble."

"I've got another idea," she said.

She gave him the rifle and put the extra mags and comm unit in his lap. And then she kissed him hard on the lips before moving behind him. She hooked her arms under his, and then he heard the grunt of effort as she hoisted him up and started dragging him across the ground.

"You're not sacrificing yourself, Hank Davidson," she said through gritted teeth. "You're getting married next week."

Hank must have blacked out because when he came to again he was propped against a wide tree trunk. She'd laid out weapons and was preparing them for battle.

"You back with me?" she asked.

"Yeah, I think so," he said. "Sorry about that."

"You weren't out long," she said, putting the comm unit in his ear and clipping the walkie-talkie to his belt.

"Listen in and tell me what they're saying," she instructed.

Hank twisted the little black dial to slightly turn up the volume to the inserted earpiece while he kept watch on Agatha. She'd strapped the rifle over her shoulder and had taken a fighting position in between him and what might be the killers' avenue of approach. She was like Rambo.

"They're speaking a mix of English and another language. But I'm not sure these guys are foreign," he said. "The last guy spoke English like a native. There was no hint of an accent."

He listened to the tone and inflexion of their communications and it appeared rushed and anxious. He had to imagine that what they thought would be a day of simply transporting a corpse had turned crummy with two of their brothers now dead.

"What are they saying?"

"I don't know, but they're not happy," he said.

"That's something, at least," Agatha said. "I hate happy killers."

Hank motioned for her to be quiet once the men launched into a stream of conversation. It wasn't a language he was familiar with. In his work with the FBI he'd dealt with many foreign nationals and international agencies.

He closed his eyes and tried to focus. There was something unusual about the pattern. His brain was fogged from the pain or he would have caught it before. There were certain words they used over and over again, almost like a code. And then it hit him.

"Navajo," he said.

"What?" Agatha asked.

"They're military," Hank said. "They're using Navajo to communicate. Like the Code Talkers during World War II."

"So the question is why would military special forces be running explosives through a failing funeral home?" she asked.

Hank rubbed his thumb and fingers together. "Money. They probably came here to wait for an evac team. It's definitely a failed mission. They've got no explosives and two dead teammates."

"Do you think they know about the explosion?" she asked.

"Who knows?" he said. "Someone could've told them or they could've seen it on the news. Maybe they're not waiting on an evac out, but they called in reinforcements to help retrieve the explosives. There's no cell service out here. They could be cut off from their contacts."

"What about Brad? Why'd they kill him if he was their mule supplier?"

"Maybe they figured the body would eventually turn

back up at the funeral home. That's the most logical place to start. Or maybe they figured the cops would be called in and everything would be traced to Brad and he'd snitch on them."

"That sounds more like Brad," Agatha said. "So they killed him to cover their tracks. I'm surprised they didn't burn the whole place down."

"They might have," Hank said. "But maybe they escaped when they heard my sisters pull up. Which means if they're waiting for reinforcements to arrive, they might be heading into Rusty Gun to clean up the rest of their mess. My sisters can identify them. And who knows who else was involved with Brad and the whole deal until we dig through all the financials. There's the potential for a lot of bodies to clean up."

"I don't know how to be G.I. Jane," Agatha said. "I can shoot with the best of them, but I'm totally out of my league in this situation. You're going to have to tell me what to do to keep us safe. They're going to search this area sooner or later. We need a plan."

He picked up the rifle and then showed her where the safety was. He didn't bother trying to explain the sight adjustments. There was no need in close-quarter combat.

"They'll find the body we just left," Hank said. "When they do, all heck is going to break loose."

"We'll be ready," Agatha said.

"I'm going to keep watch on that open field," Hank said. "As soon as they spot their downed compadre, they'll either retreat or take each side of the clearing and move into the wooded area. If one comes our way, we'll have to take the shot as he gets close."

"What about the other one?" she asked.

"I suspect once he hears gunfire, he'll head this way to

engage us. Stay put and don't give away your location with shadow breaks."

"Right," she said, her face pale and terrified in the moonlight.

"Can you climb into a tree?" he asked. "It'll give you the advantage and a better view of the area."

"It's like riding a bike, right?" she asked. "I used to be pretty good at it. Though I'd probably better start climbing. I'm older and slower than I used to be."

She leaned down to kiss him goodbye and he touched his hand to the side of her face. "Be careful. If anything ever happened to you—"

"I know," she said. "Same with you. I can't wait to be your wife."

"I love you," he said, and the chatter started once again in his earpiece. "Go. They're close. They keep saying someone's name. I'm assuming it's their dead friend."

Agatha nodded and headed off to find a good tree to climb, and Hank tried once more to get his legs to move. He was a sitting duck. And he had to make every shot count if they got in range.

He took out the earpiece and listened to the night around him, letting nature give him the warnings he needed. There was a shuffle of feet against earth, the snap of a twig, or rocks that were displaced and tumbled down into the bone yard.

He kept his eyes on where he knew they'd left the body until he saw movement in the shadows. The men stood still for a moment and then made hand signals and split up, circling around.

He heard the chatter in the earpiece and there was no need for translation. "Kill them."

CHAPTER TEN

Agatha figured out pretty quick that climbing trees wasn't like riding a bike. She didn't remember the branches stabbing her in the thighs or getting dizzy when she looked down. Every time she pulled herself up higher her ribs protested, but she kept going because she'd promised herself a long time ago that she'd never be a victim again. She'd fight hard or die trying.

The rifle slung over her shoulder kept catching on the branches, and she gave up on trying to go any higher. She estimated she was probably eight or ten feet off the ground, and she clung to the trunk and tried to maneuver herself into a position where she could get the rifle ready.

The moon was bright now, and while it helped her see out through the trees, she was sure it was equally helping the bad guys. She caught a glimpse of movement and saw one of the men disappear deeper into the trees, and she knew he was circling around behind them.

Hank would be trapped.

The stillness unnerved her. Everything went quiet. Animals, insects, people—even the wind stopped.

Hank was almost directly below her, but she couldn't see him. What she heard was the crackle from his earpiece, and if she could hear it, so could the killers. She tried to position the rifle so it rested on a tree branch, but she couldn't do it without making noise.

Hank still had his pistol and the semiautomatic 9mm that she'd removed from the man she'd killed. In hindsight, she should've held on to that pistol because it would've been much easier for her to use.

The walkie-talkie crackled again. There were no voices coming through—just white noise. She looked all around on the ground, frantic that Hank had passed out again and had pressed one of the buttons, but she couldn't see him anywhere.

Waiting in the tree was torture. She wanted to find Hank, to know he was safe. But she also knew their best chance for survival was for her to stay where she was until the time was right.

She breathed deep a couple of times and then tried to follow the path the killer would've taken. It wasn't long before she heard branches moving from below. Much too close in her opinion. He'd slithered up like a snake before she knew it.

Her heart sank. Paralyzed and possibly passed out, Hank was a sitting duck against this ruthless hunter. He was close enough she couldn't even take the safety off without him hearing. The sound would be familiar to an experienced shooter.

She held her breath until the beats of her heart drummed loudly in her ears. It was making her dizzy as she went from clear thinking to semi-panicked. The truth was, she was too old to be hanging on to a branch ten feet in the air with a rifle she wasn't sure how to shoot balanced on an unstable branch while a military special forces mercenary stalked her soon-to-be husband like a ghost in fog.

A thought popped into her head, and she acted without thinking it through. Because if she would've thought it through, she never would've gone through with it.

She waited until the man was almost directly below her and then she jumped, swinging her rifle in a long arc and smashing it against his skull. The sound of cracking bone and flesh was horrific, and she knew she'd be hearing it over and over again in her nightmares.

She landed on her feet just as he was toppling to the ground, and her legs gave way beneath her. She gagged a couple of times, and then thanked God she hadn't taken the safety off the gun. She'd have ended up shooting something and alerting the last man to her location.

Her mind began to race wildly with dark thoughts at the reality of having killed another human. She'd have done it again if it meant saving Hank's life, but she also knew she'd never forget what it felt like.

She scurried low to the ground on her hands and knees, and crawled over to the killer to check his pulse. But there was none. She stripped the man of his rifle and pistol, and turned off his walkie-talkie that was still transmitting from Hank's earpiece.

There was no time to rest. She stayed low and moved as fast as she could in between trees for cover as she searched for Hank.

"Hank, it's me," she whispered.

There was still nothing but the static from his earpiece, and she couldn't locate where the sound was coming from.

How did a paralyzed man just not be where she'd left him moments ago? She heard the crackle again and got down onto all fours, crawling around on the ground and reaching behind a tree sprouting up from a clump of bushes. She felt along the dirt and rocks until she felt the square box of the walkie-talkie and the connected earpiece. And then she turned it off.

When she'd left to climb the tree, Hank had been attached to the other end of the wires she was now holding. And now he was nowhere to be found. She closed her eyes and dropped her head to the ground.

Hank was paralyzed and hampered by cracked ribs and probably the mother of all concussions. He could only do so much. Where could he have gone? She needed to start using her head. Thinking through the problem just like she did when she was writing. There could only be so many possible outcomes.

She opened her eyes and drew in a long, cleansing breath. She needed to work the area in a grid. He hadn't even been able to move himself a few inches earlier. She stayed on the ground and started crawling out twenty paces, tracing her steps back to the man with the cracked skull. And then she set out in a different direction going another twenty paces and coming back.

She took a quick break to wipe the sweat dripping into her eyes, and then started to make another pass in the next direction. She fanned her arms back and forth as she crawled, feeling for anything, when she came across something that felt remarkably like a shoe. She patted her way across the top and squeezed, but he didn't make a sound. But then she realized he wouldn't have felt her squeezing his foot.

"Hank," she whispered.

"Not this time," a man said.

She looked up, noting the black slacks and white shirt

on her way to a very angry face. There was no talking her way out of this one. This man wanted her dead.

"Who—who are you?" she asked.

He brought his rifle up so she was staring down the barrel, and she was sure she'd never felt fear like this before.

She couldn't watch her own death, and she collapsed to the ground. All she could think was that he'd already gotten to Hank and they were going to meet again soon on the other side of the Pearly Gates.

"You should've minded your own business," he said.

She hadn't been expecting conversation so it threw her for a loop. "I'm not very good at that," she said. "I've been told that more times than I can count."

"You've got a smart mouth," he said.

"Another true statement," she said. "You're pretty good at that. I wish the media had your dedication for the truth. I don't suppose I could ask a favor."

"What?" he asked, incredulous. "No, that's ridiculous."

"I was just wondering if you wanted to shoot me in the front or the back," she said. "As a woman, I'd personally prefer the back. I'd like for my friends and family to be able to recognize me in the coffin."

He snorted a laugh. "Fine, the back it is."

"I think I deserve an explanation," she said, trying to stall.

The man threw his head back and laughed. If she'd been two hundred pounds of solid muscle she would've taken that opportunity to try and wrestle the gun away from him. But she wasn't, so she didn't.

"Why would you think that?" he asked.

"Because I single-handedly took out two of your men, and I happen to know that an old lady on the highway bagged the other. Don't you think that deserves an answer?"

He growled, the laughter gone. "That's going to make killing you so much more satisfying."

"That's a little dramatic," Agatha said. "I'm a writer, so I know a thing or two about pacing." She had no idea what came over her. It's like she'd just resigned herself to her upcoming death, and if there was even the smallest fraction of a chance that Hank was still alive she wanted to give him time to take cover.

"All I'm saying is you guys aren't too hard to profile. Disgruntled military. Probably dishonorably discharged. And what, you decide you're owed a little something extra for your service so being a mercenary sounds like a good idea. Only you're not that great at it. And you hook up with someone like Brad Hartley who's never done a right thing in his life. That's a losing team if I've ever heard one."

"Shut up," he said, his anger growing wilder, and he nudged her in the forehead with the rifle.

"No," she said calmly. "And then you let a van full of old ladies best you and steal your body. I guess it wasn't worth sticking around to find out if the bomb was going to detonate with their van sitting on top of it."

"How'd you know about the bomb?" he asked.

"Because it blew the morgue to heck and back," Agatha said. "You killed three people, there are witnesses, and all your buddies are dead so there's no one to talk code to. Do you really thing you're going to come out of this on top?"

"You're smart," he said. "You just come up with all that?"

"Of course not," she said, improvising. "Everyone who's worked this case knows all that. You guys are not good at your jobs. You should probably get in a different line of work. You've got the whole alphabet soup of agencies looking for you."

"Well then," he said. "It looks like I need to get going. Don't worry, I'm sure they'll find your body in the morning."

"One last question," she asked. "Why Brad Hartley?"

"Him?" the man snorted. "Easy. He needed the cash and we needed the facility. It was a sweet deal. Until it wasn't. Brad liked to siphon money into his own little hidey-holes. We weren't amused."

"How long have y'all been working with Brad? It's not easy to go unnoticed in a place like Rusty Gun."

"Because we don't go to him," the guy said. "He comes to us. We've been here almost a year. No one ever comes out here."

"So you guys and Brad are just drones. No way you're at the head of this. Who's the big cheese? Who's paying you?"

"Time's up, buttercup," he said, not answering the questions.

He pulled the stock of his rifle against his shoulder and looked down the barrel. Agatha closed her eyes, and all she could think was that she'd never gotten to start the rest of her life with Hank.

Bang!

Agatha collapsed onto the ground.

***

The smoke cleared, and Hank kept his weapon trained on the man who had planned to kill Agatha in cold blood. It hadn't been the first time he'd had to take a life, but he knew it would be the first time he'd have no remorse over the taking of a life.

His chest tightened as he looked at Agatha crumpled on the ground, and just for a second, he wondered if he'd made the shot too late.

"Agatha," Hank said, trying to maneuver his body closer. "Agatha, wake up. It's me. You're okay."

He saw her hand twitch and breathed out a sigh of relief.

"It's me, baby. Are you okay?" he asked again.

She turned her head slowly, her eyes dazed and her face pale. "Hank?" she asked, and then she smiled. "I knew I'd see you again. But this is not how I imagined heaven would look."

"You're not dead, baby," he said. "I can't move, or I'd be there holding you in my arms. You scared me to death."

A little life came into her eyes, and she pushed up off the ground. Dirt and leaves and twigs stuck out from her hair, dirt smudged her face, and her clothes were torn. She'd never looked more beautiful.

She looked at the body lying inches from her and then looked back at Hank. And then her whole body started to shake, and she scooted away from him as fast as she could.

"How?" she asked. "I don't understand. I'm not dead?"

"No, you're fine," Hank assured her.

He saw the change in her—relief, panic, anger, and desperation—and then she clawed her way across the leaves and threw herself into his arms. Their bodies were bruised and battered, but they were alive, and he wasn't sure he'd be able to let her go.

"You're okay," she sobbed. She traced her hands along his cheeks and then hugged him again.

"I'm not leaving you," Hank said. "We've got a lot of life left in front of us."

"I thought he'd shot me," she said. "I knew I was dead."

"I had a bead on him the whole time," Hank assured her. "But I needed him to clear the tree before I had a clear shot. Fortunately, your goading him worked and he inched forward just enough for me to get him. What were you thinking? I almost went out of my mind when I heard you taunting him like that."

"I don't know," she said. "I wasn't scared. Not then. I think it's all catching up to me now." Her teeth chattered and she hugged him harder.

"I couldn't find you," she said.

"I had to move, so I left the walkie-talkie as a distraction in hopes of luring the killer to it. I rolled over to the right until I smashed into this tree, and decided it was as good a place as any to wait. Not that moving was an option. I was close enough to hear you crack that other guy's skull."

She winced. "Don't remind me. Please tell me he's the last of them. I can't take any more of this."

He recognized the signs of a breakdown. It was common following high-stress situations. His bride-to-be had just taken out two mercenaries before almost being killed herself. Hank knew it would take more than keeping her mind on the upcoming wedding to get her through the trauma she'd been through.

"He's the last of the four," Hank said. "But I don't think this ends with them. We'll have to see how this shakes out once the investigation is started. But they were expecting company. Someone was supposed to come and extract them."

A look of terror etched across her face.

"We've got to get out of here," she said. "Now."

"You hear that?" Hank asked, listening to the *whump, whump, whump* of chopper blades getting closer. "The cavalry is finally here. I don't think we need to worry about any others right now.

"Thank God," Agatha said, moving to stand up and get their attention.

"Stay close, baby. I'm not ready to let you go just yet," Hank said. "I turned on my tracker on my phone. They'll find us."

EPILOGUE

Saturday

Hank's hospital room was packed with well-wishers, flowers, and balloons. Someone had even managed to sneak him in a meatball sandwich, and a full bag of little candy bars. Hank's sweet tooth was legendary.

Agatha stayed close to his bed as his sisters fussed around him. They loved him, there was no question of that. And she and Hank had already decided the best way to deal with them was to set boundaries. If they wanted to be part of their life, then they'd have to behave. The ball was in their court.

Betty stroked the bottoms of his feet in hopes she would generate a feeling or response, and Patsy kept checking the machines, making sure he was getting the correct doses. She was a retired nurse, so she was determined not to let anything slip by her notice. Brenda kept a watchful eye on Agatha while Hazel stood guard at the door.

Agatha knew there was a law against having firearms in the hospital, but if she were a betting woman, she'd say they were probably all packing heat.

Hank was having a hushed conversation with Coil, Will Ellis, and Jason Whitehorse, but Agatha had tuned out. They were trying to persuade Hank to take it easy and rest, and let them handle the rest of the case. Hank had that stubborn look on his face, so she knew how the conversation would end. And so did Coil, Ellis, and Whitehorse. Sometimes she thought men just liked to argue.

Jimmy James's funeral arrangements were being handled by the Rangers' Honor Guard Section, and they were preparing a full police funeral memorial service. Nothing that had happened had really sunk in yet. But she felt like she was a string pulled too tight.

Besides his sisters and Coil, Whitehorse, and Ellis, Karl and Heather had stopped by, and Rodriguez and Springer were standing in the doorway because there was just no more room.

The chatter rose until the serious-looking man with wrinkles on his forehead and round glasses walked into the room with his official starched white jacket and a handful of papers. Dr. Sullivan was always courteous, but he had yet to deliver any optimistic news over the last two days. If he told her to wait and see one more time, she couldn't be held responsible for her actions.

"This looks like a party," Dr. Sullivan said. "Why wasn't I invited?"

"You're always welcome, Doc," Hank said, straining to pull himself into an upright position.

"How you feeling today, Hank?"

Hank rubbed his ribs and grimaced. "Sore around the middle. Otherwise, I'm feeling pretty good."

"I'd feel better too if I'd just eaten a meatball sub."

Hank grinned sheepishly.

"As far as the pain around the middle, those ribs are

pretty battered. You know the drill. We can bind them, but they'll heal on their own. You and Ms. Agatha can help bind each other."

"I'm feeling much better as long as I don't move," Agatha said.

"That should make y'all's wedding real interesting. My wife and I can't wait to come. Thanks for the invite, by the way."

"The more the merrier," Hank said. "No more stalling, Doc. Tell me what's going on with my legs."

"Well—" Dr. Sullivan paused and looked at everyone in the room.

"Go on," Hank said. "They're my family."

"Your prognosis hasn't gotten any better," he said. "But it also hasn't gotten any worse."

"How much worse can it get than being paralyzed?" Agatha asked.

Hank took her hand and squeezed.

"We suspect that the swelling around the base of your spinal after you fell is what caused the paralysis. And we've not been able to get an accurate picture of the extent of the spinal damage because of the swelling. We'll keep running tests and trying to get the swelling down, but I'm sorry, that's all I can give you right now."

"Do you think it's permanent?" Hank asked.

"I'm just not comfortable making a determination this soon. Once the swelling subsides, we'll know much more, but until then, I can't say one way or the other."

"What are you most worried about?" Agatha asked him.

"Well," Sullivan said. "It's been two days, and a lot of times the patient will start to feel a tingling sensation like when your arm or leg fall asleep. Anything yet?"

"I've almost worn a rut in the bottom of his foot," Betty said. "His legs haven't even twitched."

Sullivan nodded and made a note in his chart.

"What should we do?" Hank asked.

"Honestly, the best thing you can do is run everyone out of this room. Rest is what makes the difference. I know you're lying down, but all of this interaction isn't the type of rest that heals the body."

"Consider it done," Agatha said. "Anything else?"

"Focus on your upcoming marriage," he said. "The body heals at the speed it wants to. We can help it with medicine, but worry and anxiety slow the process. Keep making plans, and keep thinking about your futures."

"Does that mean I can go home soon?"

"You're going to require continued care as long as the paralysis stays, but you won't be confined here. Maybe a couple of more days, and then we can get you set up with everything you need at home."

"Thanks, Doc," Hank said, smiling. He'd never wanted his own bed so bad in his life.

"And Agatha," Sullivan said. "That order for everyone to clear out goes for you too. You haven't had any sleep since you've been here, and your injuries aren't exactly a walk in the park. You need rest, food, and then more rest. Doctor's orders.'

"Okay, you heard the man," Coil said. "Everybody out."

"Thanks Coil," Hank said, and then pulled his friend down and spoke in a low voice. "Keep an eye on Agatha, will you? I don't think this has hit her yet."

"Always."

"Come on, honey," Heather said. "I'll drive you back, and Karl can catch a ride back to the station."

"We're going back to the hotel," Hazel said. "But we're sticking around. Call us if you need anything."

Hank nodded. "I will. Promise. I love you all."

He noticed his sisters all teared up at the declaration. Those words hadn't been uttered often in their home growing up.

After everyone was out of the room, Agatha leaned down to kiss Hank. "I'll be back in the morning."

"Not too early," he said. "Get some sleep. And if you're not tired, go find something to do. I'm sure Heather can keep you occupied until you pass out from exhaustion."

"Come on, girl," Heather said, poking her head back in the room.

"I'm coming," Agatha said.

She kissed Hank and they held each other tighter than they'd ever held on to one another. It was breaking her heart to leave him, but she knew it was best to let him rest.

"Heather got my phone fixed, so text me anytime," she said.

Hank gave a thumbs-up and his eyes fluttered closed.

The drive back to Rusty Gun was mostly quiet. Agatha preferred the silence while Heather had always been the chatty one. It had been that way ever since the Cartwright family had moved to town.

"Do you want me to take you home?" she asked. "Those bags under your eyes could hold a milk jug."

"No," Agatha said. "I'm not tired. I'm restless. And I don't want to sit at home by myself remembering what happened."

"Leave it to me, girl. I've got just the thing. We had to miss our spa day at Gloria's yesterday, but I bet if I ask real nice and pay her double she'll get us in lickety-split. Besides, she needs the money. She's a single mom, and her side jobs aren't real reliable. I guess now that the funeral home is shut down, she'll have to go back to waiting tables."

"The funeral home?"

"She does hair and makeup for all the dead people," Heather said. "She's real talented. I hardly recognized Mr. Oglesby when I saw him last month. He never looked that good when he was living."

Heather pulled into the parking lot of Gloria's Day Spa, but there was only one other car in the lot. The open sign flashed in the window.

"Not much business," Agatha said.

"She's been trying to hire more stylists and technicians," Heather said. "It's real nice on the inside. As nice as any of the spas I've been to in the city. But she works strictly on appointments, and people in Rusty Gun are more of the walk-in crowd. Come on."

They got out of the car and Agatha pushed the door open to the front of the salon.

"Gloria, your favorite client is here," Heather said cheerfully. "We want the works."

"I don't think she's here," Agatha said, looking around the empty salon. Heather was right, it was as nice as any she'd seen. Very high quality, and the water feature behind the front desk was mesmerizing.

"Gloria?" Heather asked again. "You with a client?"

Agatha walked down the hallway where the treatment rooms were, but all the doors were open. The last door on the left was an office, and it was the only one where the door was half open.

Agatha pushed it the rest of the way, but it caught on something. She pushed harder and a bloody hand flopped out onto the carpet.

"Heather," Agatha said. "I don't think Gloria is available today."

NEXT UP: FIST COMES DEATH, THEN COMES MARRIAGE

JULY 2020

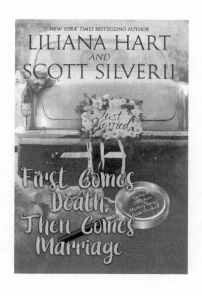

ORDER TODAY

Liliana and I have loved sharing these stories in our Harley & Davidson Mystery Series with you.

There are many more adventures to be had for Aggie and Hank. Make sure you stay up to date with life in Rusty Gun, Texas by signing up for our emails.

Thanks again and please be sure to leave a review where you bought each story and, recommend the series to your friends.

Kindly,
Scott & Liliana

Enjoy this book? You can make a big difference

Reviews are so important in helping us get the word out about Harley and Davidson Mystery Series. If you've enjoyed this adventure Liliana & I would be so grateful if you would take a few minutes to leave a review (it can be as short as you like) on the book's buy page.

Thanks,
Scott & Liliana

ACKNOWLEDGMENTS

Always a very special Thank You to our cover design artist Dar Albert at Wicked Smart Designs. The Best. Editor. Ever. Imogen Howson, we appreciate dearly.

ALSO BY LILIANA HART & LOUIS SCOTT

Books by Liliana Hart and Louis Scott

The Harley and Davidson Mystery Series

The Farmer's Slaughter

A Tisket a Casket

I Saw Mommy Killing Santa Claus

Get Your Murder Running

Deceased and Desist

Malice in Wonderland

Tequila Mockingbird

Gone With the Sin

Grime and Punishment

Blazing Rattles

A Salt and Battery

Curl Up and Dye

First Comes Death Then Comes Marriage

Box Set 1 (Books 1 - 4)

Box Set 2 (Books 5 - 8)

ABOUT LILIANA HART

Liliana Hart is a New York Times, USAToday, and Publisher's Weekly bestselling author of more than sixty titles. After starting her first novel her freshman year of college, she immediately became addicted to writing and knew she'd found what she was meant to do with her life. She has no idea why she majored in music.

Since publishing in June 2011, Liliana has sold more than six-million books. All three of her series have made multiple appearances on the New York Times list.

Liliana can almost always be found at her computer writing, hauling five kids to various activities, or spending time with her husband. She calls Texas home.

If you enjoyed reading *this*, I would appreciate it if you would help others enjoy this book, too.

Lend it. This e-book is lending-enabled, so please, share it with a friend.

Recommend it. Please help other readers find this book by recommending it to friends, readers' groups and discussion boards.

Review it. Please tell other readers why you liked this book by reviewing. If you do write a review, please send me an email at lilianahartauthor@gmail.com, or visit me at http://www.lilianahart.com.

Connect with me online:
www.lilianahart.com
lilianahartauthor@gmail.com

facebook.com/LilianaHart

instagram.com/LilianaHart

bookbub.com/authors/liliana-hart

ABOUT LOUIS SCOTT

Liliana's writing partner and husband, Scott blends over 25 years of heart-stopping policing Special Operations experience.

From deep in the heart of south Louisiana's Cajun Country, his action-packed writing style is seasoned by the Mardi Gras, hurricanes and crawfish étouffée.

Don't let the easy Creole smile fool you. The author served most of a highly decorated career in SOG buying dope, banging down doors, and busting bad guys.

Bringing characters to life based on those amazing experiences, Scott writes it like he lived it.

Lock and Load – Let's Roll.

Made in the USA
Middletown, DE
31 May 2021